S0-ABZ-262

"You're all business, aren't you, Miss Liz?"

"It's Mrs. Gentry," she corrected. "And I do try to act like a professional when I'm having a business meeting."

"Of course," Todd said, responding to her cool demeanor with a touch of sarcasm. The woman infuriated him. Worse, she confused him. While the prim set of her mouth confirmed his image of a straitlaced schoolmarm, he felt like kissing those lips until they were bruised and swollen and parted on a sigh of pleasure.

"Why are you so nervous around me?" he asked suddenly.

She paled and said staunchly, "I am not nervous!"

"Oh, really? Do you always destroy paperclips that way?"

Liz looked down at her desk. There was indeed a pile of twisted bits of metal in front of her. "I'll repeat myself, Mr. Lewis. You don't make me nervous. Not at all."

But they both knew it was a lie.

Dear Reader,

Happy New Year, and many thanks for the notes and letters you've sent to the authors and editors of Silhouette **Special Edition** over the past twelve months. Although we seldom have time to write individual responses, I'd like to take this opportunity to let you know how much we value all your comments. Your praise and plaudits warm our hearts and give our efforts meaning; your questions and suggestions keep us on our toes as we continually strive to make each of our six monthly Silhouette **Special Edition** novels a truly significant romance-reading event.

Our authors and editors believe you deserve writing of the highest caliber, satisfying novelistic scope, and a profound emotional experience with each book you read. Your letters tell us that you've come to trust Silhouette **Special Edition** to deliver romance fiction of that quality, depth, and sensitivity time and time again. With the advent of the new year, we're renewing a pledge: to do our very best, month after month, edition after edition, to continue bringing you "romance you can believe in."

On behalf of all the authors and editors of Silhouette **Special Edition**,

Thanks again and best wishes,

Leslie Kazanjian,
Senior Editor

P.S. This month, ask your bookseller for *The Forever Rose*, a new historical novel by one of your Silhouette **Special Edition** favorites, Curtiss Ann Matlock—the author has promised "family ties" to her next two contemporary novels, coming this year from Silhouette **Special Edition**!

SHERRYL WOODS
Miss Liz's Passion

Silhouette Special Edition

Published by Silhouette Books New York

America's Publisher of Contemporary Romance

Acknowledgments

Although Dolphin Reach, the characters, and the incidents in *Miss Liz's Passion* are fiction, a similarly innovative program is currently under way at the Dolphin Research Center in Grassy Key, Florida. A special thanks to Dr. David Nathanson for sharing his expertise, to the enthusiastic Dolphin Research Center staff and to Spring and her family for sharing their time and enthusiasm.

For Moira, who brings dedication, imagination and love to some very special students

SILHOUETTE BOOKS
300 East 42nd St., New York, N.Y. 10017

Copyright © 1990 by Sherryl Woods

All rights reserved. Except for use in any review, the reproduction or utilization of this work in whole or in part in any form by any electronic, mechanical or other means, now known or hereafter invented, including xerography, photocopying and recording, or in any information storage or retrieval system, is forbidden without the permission of Silhouette Books, 300 E. 42nd St., New York, N.Y. 10017

ISBN: 0-373-09573-2

First Silhouette Books printing January 1990

All the characters in this book are fictitious. Any resemblance to actual persons, living or dead, is purely coincidental.

®: Trademark used under license and registered in the United States Patent and Trademark Office and in other countries.

Printed in the U.S.A.

Books by Sherryl Woods

Silhouette Desire

Not at Eight, Darling #309
Yesterday's Love #329
Come Fly with Me #345
A Gift of Love #375
Can't Say No #431
Heartland #472
One Touch of Moondust #521

Silhouette Special Edition

Safe Harbor #425
Never Let Go #446
Edge of Forever #484
In Too Deep #522
Miss Liz's Passion #573

SHERRYL WOODS

lives by the ocean, which, she says, provides daily inspiration for the romance in her soul. She further explains that her years as a television critic taught her about steamy plots and humor; her years as a travel editor took her to exotic locations; and her years as a crummy weekend tennis player taught her to stick with what she enjoyed most—writing. "What better way is there," Sherryl asks, "to combine all that experience than by creating romantic stories?"

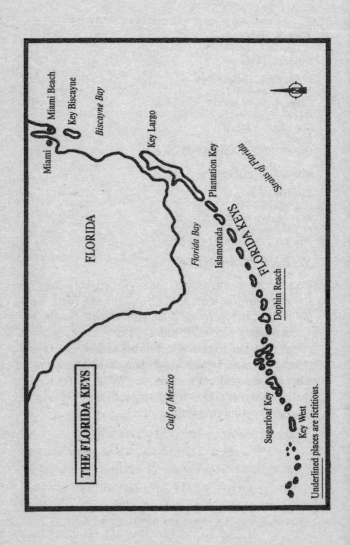

THE FLORIDA KEYS

FLORIDA

Miami
Miami Beach
Key Biscayne
Biscayne Bay
Key Largo
Plantation Key
Islamorada
Florida Bay
FLORIDA KEYS
Straits of Florida
Dolphin Reach
Gulf of Mexico
Sugarloaf Key
Key West

Underlined places are fictitious.

Prologue

The bite mark was an angry red, only one shade darker than Teri Lynn's face as she howled at the top of her lungs and clutched her injured arm. Breathless from streaking across the grassy playground to break up the fight, Liz Gentry knelt between the crying girl and her eight-year-old tormentor.

"Kevin, what is the meaning of this?" Liz demanded as she wiped away Teri Lynn's tears with a lace-edged, lavender-scented handkerchief.

The towheaded boy she addressed stared sullenly at the ground, scuffing the toe of his sneaker back and forth in the dirt. She put a firm hand on his chin and forced him to meet her gaze. "Kevin?"

She sighed as he remained obstinately silent.

"He bit me, Mrs. Gentry. For no reason, he just bit me," Teri Lynn said between sobs.

"Did not," Kevin muttered defiantly.

"Did, too." Teri Lynn insisted with a sniff as she inched closer to Liz's side.

"Kevin, if you didn't do it, who did?" Liz asked impatiently, then sighed again.

Of course, Kevin had done it. She'd seen him herself. One minute he and Teri Lynn had been tossing a ball back and forth on the playground. Seconds later he had flown at her in a rage. Half a dozen shocked classmates had stared on silently, while others, seemingly immune to Kevin's displays of temper, continued with their noisy games.

So much for her hopes for an uneventful recess, she thought as she comforted Teri Lynn. Thanks to Kevin, at the rate the school year was going, she would have had a quieter time of it in the Marines.

As the bell rang ending recess, she surveyed the combatants. Both of them had cuts and scrapes, but that bite mark on Teri Lynn's arm was the worst injury.

"Okay, we won't argue about it now. Teri Lynn, I'll take you to the school nurse as soon as I get the rest of the class inside. Kevin, you and I will discuss this after school. In the meantime, you will go to the principal's office and wait for me."

Her tone left no room for argument. Not that Kevin would have given her one. He simply nodded as he always did. Inside the building, as she watched, he walked down the deserted hall and turned into the office. She knew from experience she would find him there at the end of the school day, sitting on a bench, his expression stoic. Only the telltale traces of tears on his cheeks ever offered any indication that he'd found the recurring incidents of misbehavior or the punishment upsetting.

The last hours of school dragged on interminably. She tried to listen as the students read their English assignments aloud, but she couldn't get her mind off Kevin. Despite his troublesome behavior, something about the child's lost, world-weary expression tugged at her heart. She cared about all of her students. She loved the challenge of making them respond, of making learning exciting for them. With Kevin the challenge had been doubled because her usual methods had failed so miserably. Whether it was her own ego or Kevin's apparent need, he had gotten to her in a way that none of the other students had.

But how on earth was she going to handle this ongoing behavior problem? No matter how compassionately she felt toward Kevin, his conduct had to be corrected. There was a fight or a temper tantrum, or a sulking retreat almost every day. The child clearly needed help, more help than she could possibly offer him in a room crowded with thirty-five energetic third-graders.

It was only the first month of school and already she had repeatedly sent notes home to his father, who had sole custody for reasons not made clear in the file. No mention was made of the mother. In her first letter to Todd Lewis she had explained Kevin's behavior prob-

lems in depth, detailing her suspicions about the cause
and requesting a meeting to discuss solutions. The
second note and the third had been a little more impatient, a little more concise. Admittedly, the last one
had been barely polite.

Todd Lewis had yet to call, much less appear, which
told her quite a lot about the man's indifference to his
son's well-being and left her thoroughly frustrated.
Reaching him by phone had been no more successful.
With an increasing sense of urgency, she had left at
least half a dozen messages on his home answering
machine in the last two days. If he had a business
number, she couldn't find it. The emergency number
in the file had turned out to belong to a neighbor, who
looked out for Kevin after school. Liz had been unwilling to draw the woman into the midst of the problem. She had asked her only to relay a message asking
Todd Lewis to call. The woman had agreed readily
enough, but admitted she rarely saw him.

Liz resolved to try just once more to arrange a
meeting. If the man failed to show up yet again, she
would have to resort to stronger action. There were
authorities she could ask to intercede. Filled with indignation on Kevin's behalf, she dismissed the class,
asked the teacher next door to get her students to their
buses, then wrote the harshest note yet, hoping to
shake Todd Lewis from his parental apathy.

When she'd finished the note, she went to get Kevin.
As she'd expected, he was sitting on the wooden bench
in the office, his short legs sticking out in front of him,
his hands folded in his lap. He didn't even look up as

she sat down beside him. She was torn between wanting to hug him or shake him. He looked as though he desperately needed a hug.

"Okay, Kevin. Let's talk about this for a few minutes before you catch the school bus. Tell me what happened out there this afternoon," she began quietly.

He shook his head, his expression hopeless. That look broke her heart. No child of eight should have eyes that devoid of hope.

"Why not?" she probed.

"Doesn't matter," he said in a voice so soft she had to lean down to hear him.

"It does matter. Fighting is no way to settle an argument."

"Teri Lynn started it," he said with more spirit.

"Kevin, I was watching. I saw you knock her down."

"Only because—"

"Because what?"

His chin set stubbornly.

"Kevin?"

"She said something," he mumbled.

"What?"

He shook his head again.

"Kevin, this is not the first fight you've had. I can't help, if you won't tell me what the fights are about. I don't want to recommend that you be suspended, but that's where you're heading."

Blue eyes shimmering with tears blinked wide at her stern tone. Liz felt her heart constrict. If only she could get to the bottom of this. Her voice softened. "Honey, please, what did she say that made you so mad?"

His lower lip trembled. Liz waited as he started to speak, swallowed hard, then tried again. "She-she . . . said . . ."

"Come on, sweetheart. You can tell me."

His shoulders slumped and tears spilled down his cheeks. "She said I was a . . . a d-dummy."

Liz felt the sting of salty tears in her own eyes at the note of despair she heard in his voice. He believed it! This bright, outgoing child believed he was a failure because of the cruel taunts of a classmate and her own inability to find teaching methods that would reach him.

Kevin needed diagnostic testing. He needed special classes. Most of all, he needed a father who loved him enough to see that the answers to his learning dilemma were found before Kevin withdrew into himself entirely. Damn Todd Lewis!

More than ever, she was glad that this latest note had been worded so strongly. The man's indifference was appalling. Furious, she decided if he failed to respond this time it would be the last. She renewed her vow to set in motion whatever regulations were necessary to see that Kevin got the help that would enable him to learn. More important, she would see that something was done to restore his rapidly deteriorating self-esteem.

"Kevin, you are not a dummy," she said with every ounce of conviction she could manage. "You are a very smart little boy."

He regarded her doubtfully. "But you're always correcting me. That's why Teri Lynn said it. She says you don't like me, that nobody likes me because I always make mistakes." He sighed heavily. "And I do. I can't get nothing right."

"Anything," she corrected instinctively, then could have bitten her tongue. Why just this once couldn't she have let a mistake slide? "Honey, I do like you. I know this is hard for you to understand, but I believe that the reason you make mistakes is not because you're not very, very smart, but because you have something called a learning disability. That's what I want to talk to your father about. I think we should do some tests to find out why it's so hard for you to learn."

"Is that what the note says?" he asked, fingering the sealed envelope suspiciously.

She considered the note's indignant comments. For a fleeting instant she was almost grateful that Kevin had difficulty reading. "More or less," she said wryly. "Kevin, is there some reason your father hasn't been able to come in when I've asked him to?"

He stared at the floor and shook his head. "I don't know. He's pretty busy, I guess." There was an obvious note of pride in his voice as he added, "He works real hard."

"You just tell him that I expect to see him tomorrow. Okay?"

"I'll tell him." He frowned. "You're not gonna be mad at him for not coming before, are you?"

Liz struggled to keep her tone impassive. "Don't worry about that. We'll work things out and once your dad and I talk I'm sure things will get better for you. Now run along before you miss the early bus again today."

He was on his feet at once, his natural exuberance restored.

"Kevin!"

He glanced back at her. "We'll discuss your apology to Teri Lynn in the morning."

He nodded once, shot her a cheerful grin and was out the door, leaving her to ponder exactly how many years she would spend in jail if she tarred and feathered Todd Lewis.

Chapter One

The neat, handwritten letter had all the primness of some Victorian maiden's blush. According to the indignant opening line, it was not the first such reprimand that Todd Lewis should have received in the past month. The prissy, uptight tone might have amused him had the contents not infuriated him so.

Exhausted by an endless and frustrating day under the hot Miami sun, he reached for the can of beer beside his chair. Perhaps he was overreacting. God knows, it would be understandable. He was bone-weary. His shoulders ached, his back felt like someone was holding a burning knife in the middle of it and his thighs throbbed from the strain of struggling with those damned girders since just after dawn. He had little patience left for someone who'd spent a few hours lolling around in an air-conditioned classroom and still had complaints about how tough the workday was.

He took a long swallow of beer, then slowly read the letter again. The words and the crisp, precise, censuring tone hadn't mellowed one whit. Neither did his dark mood.

Elizabeth Gentry—he was willing to bet it was *Miss* Gentry—was sharply criticizing his son. For some reason he couldn't quite follow, she didn't seem to be too thrilled with him, either. She demanded that Todd come in the following afternoon at 3:30 to discuss the boy's "uncontrollable behavior, deplorable manners and inappropriate language."

Todd felt his blood pressure begin to soar again. He did not appreciate being chastised in such a demeaning tone by a woman he'd never even met. Nor was he wild about the labels she'd slapped on his son. Another sip of beer soothed his parched throat but not his fiery temper.

He could just picture the woman. Gray hair drawn back in a tidy little bun, a spine of steel, no makeup, rimless glasses sliding down to the end of her too-large nose, nondescript clothes in gray or brown or maybe one of those little floral prints his grandmother used to wear. He sighed at the daunting prospect. He had no idea how to deal with a sexless, unimaginative woman like that.

He took another sip of beer and read on. "Your continued refusal to take action in this matter indicates a startling lack of interest in Kevin's educational well-being and social adjustment. Should you fail to keep this appointment, I am afraid it will be necessary for me to pursue the matter with other authorities.''

What other authorities? Was the woman actually suggesting that he be reported to some local bureaucrat, maybe even a state agency? A knot formed in his stomach at the insulting suggestion that he was an uncaring father, who approved of—what was it?— *uncontrollable behavior, deplorable manners and inappropriate language.*

Okay, he was willing to admit that Kevin was a handful, but what eight-year-old wasn't? He just needed a little firm discipline every now and then.

Suddenly the nagging memory of his ex-wife's endless complaints about Kevin's manageability returned with untimely clarity. He'd dismissed her rantings at the time as yet another excuse for walking out on them. Sarah had wanted to leave long before the night she'd finally packed her bags and departed. She'd been too young, too immature to accept the responsibility of marriage, much less a troublesome son. He had blamed the inability to cope on her, not Kevin.

The comparison gave him a moment's pause, but he dismissed the significance almost at once. No doubt this terribly proper and probably ancient Miss Gentry was equally inept with children. If she couldn't handle an eight-year-old boy, perhaps she'd chosen the wrong profession. Perhaps she should be teaching piano and embroidery to sedate young ladies in frilly dresses and dainty white gloves, instead of third-grade boys who got dirt on their clothes even before the school bus picked them up in the morning.

He glanced across the room at his sturdy, blond son. Kevin was quietly racing small cars through an intricately designed village he'd built from the set of Lego blocks he'd begged for and received for his birthday. Todd figured the subdued behavior would last no more than another ten minutes, long enough for his son to feel secure that this note from his teacher would not result in some sort of punishment.

"Kevin." He kept his tone determinedly neutral. Still, wary blue eyes glanced up from the toy Porsche that was about to skitter around the village's sharpest turn. A tiny jaw jutted up, mimicking all too accurately Todd's own frequently belligerent expression. That look warned him that there just might be something behind Miss Gentry's complaints.

"What's this all about, son?"

"Same old stuff." Kevin directed his attention back to the car. It whizzed around the turn and up a hill.

"What stuff?" Todd persisted. "I gather this is not the first time your teacher has written."

A guilty blush spread across Kevin's round, freckled cheeks and he continued to look down. Todd nodded with sudden understanding. No wonder the teacher had been indignant. She thought he'd seen all of her earlier notes and had intentionally ignored them.

"I see," he said wearily. "What did you do with the other letters?"

There was the tiniest hesitation before Kevin said in a whisper, "I lost 'em."

"Really? How convenient," he said, barely controlling his temper. "Suppose you tell me what they were about."

Kevin studied the miniature red Porsche he was pushing back and forth and mumbled, "She said she told you in this one."

"I want to hear it from you."

Kevin remained stubbornly silent. Todd knew from experience that getting him to talk now was going to require tact and patience. He was shorter than usual on both tonight.

"Son, she says this is the fifth note in the last three weeks. Are you sure there's not something happening in school that you should tell me about?"

Kevin's expression turned increasingly defiant. "I told you, Dad. She don't like me. That's all it is."

"School just started a month ago. Why would you think your teacher doesn't like you?"

"Everybody knows it, Dad. She's always telling me how to do stuff."

Despite himself, Todd grinned. "She's a teacher. That's what teachers do."

"Yeah, but Dad, she only tells *me*. Even when I tell her I can't do it, she makes me. The other kids get it, but I can't. I try, Dad. Really."

The tears that welled up despite the tough facade convinced Todd that his son was telling the truth, at least as he saw it. A swift surge of compassion swept through him, blotting out for a moment his need to get

to the bottom of the teacher's complaints. His overwhelming desire to protect Kevin at any cost refueled
his anger at the stiff, unyielding Miss Gentry and gave
substance to all of his long-standing suspicions about
the school system's ineptitude. It had done a lousy
enough job with him. He'd obviously been foolish to
hope that things had improved.

What kind of teacher would single out a child day
after day like that? He'd tried his darnedest not to in-
terfere, to let the school do what it was supposed to
do—educate his son, but he wouldn't have the boy
made out to be some sort of freak because he was a
little slower than the other kids. Kevin was smart as a
whip. Anyone who took the time to talk to him could
see that.

"Are you going to talk to her, Dad?" Kevin's voice
was hesitant, the tone a heartbreaking mix of hope-
fulness and fear. Todd wasn't sure what response his
son really wanted.

"Don't you want me to?" he asked, though he
knew there was no longer any real choice in the matter.

Kevin shrugged, but his little shoulders were
slumped so dejectedly it made Todd feel like pounding his fist through a wall. "She's made me stay after
school almost every day this week," Kevin finally admitted. "A couple of times I almost missed the bus. I
think she's real mad at both of us now."

Todd sighed. Kevin tried so hard not to let anyone
fight his battles for him. If only he'd told Todd sooner,
perhaps this wouldn't have gotten so far out of hand.

The prospect of confronting Miss Gentry's self-righteous antagonism held about as much appeal as putting in another grueling, mishap-ridden twelve-hour day at the site of his latest shopping mall.

"Then maybe it's time I have a talk with her," he said, anyway. "Don't worry about it, son. I'll get it straightened out. Tell her I'll be there tomorrow afternoon." He recalled the string of problems he'd left behind at the construction site and the imperious tone of that note, then amended, "Or the next day, at the latest."

But despite the reassurance, fear still flickered in Kevin's eyes. That frightened expression aroused all of Todd's fierce protective instincts. He remembered every single humiliating moment of his own school experience and swore to himself that Miss Elizabeth Gentry would not put his son through the same sort of torment.

Liz stared longingly out the classroom window at the swaying palm trees and deep blue sky. It was a perfect Florida day. The humidity had vanished on the breeze. She had only five more spelling papers to grade before she could leave the confining classroom and enjoy what was left of the early October afternoon. The prospect of a long swim raised her spirits considerably.

She had had an absolutely hellish day again. The school had instituted yet another form that had to be filled out, though no one knew quite why. Two of her students had been sent home with the flu, after generously sharing their germs, no doubt. She'd had cafeteria duty, which almost always left her with a headache. Today's was still throbbing at the base of her skull. And Kevin had gotten into another fight. This time he'd sent Cindy Jamison to the school nurse with a bloody lip. She herself had gotten a lump on her shin and a run in her hose trying to break up the brawl.

Now Kevin was sitting at his desk, his head bent over another assignment as they waited for his father, who was already forty minutes late. The man probably had no intention of showing up this time, either, though Kevin had vowed that he would be here.

She heard a soft, snuffling sound and looked back just in time to catch sight of a tear spilling onto Kevin's paper. Her heart constricted. Blast that stubborn, indifferent father of his.

"Kevin, bring me your paper."

He looked up, his expression so woebegone that once again she felt like taking his father apart piece by piece.

When Kevin didn't move, she said, "Aren't you finished?"

He shook his head.

"That's okay. Show me what you have and we'll do the rest together."

"It's not very good."

"No problem. We'll work on it."

Kevin approached her desk with the look of a child being told that Santa Claus was leaving him only a lump of coal. It was an expression without hope. Stoic and resigned, he placed the rumpled page in front of her. "I made a lot of mistakes."

"Then let's see what we can do about them," she said briskly. "You know everybody makes mistakes when they tackle something new. It's nothing to be ashamed of and it's definitely no reason not to at least try."

Kevin regarded her with surprise. "My dad says that, too."

Liz was startled that they'd even discussed the subject. Her image of Todd Lewis did not include supportive father-son talks. She'd been certain that he either ignored the boy altogether or pressured him by expecting perfection.

"Does your dad help you with your homework?"

"Sometimes," Kevin said evasively. "Mostly Mrs. Henley helps me." Mrs. Henley was the woman next door.

"Sometimes, if Dad's real late, she fixes dinner and helps me with my homework."

Liz felt that familiar surge of helplessness rush through her again. For the next half hour she and Kevin worked on correcting his paper. It was a tedious, frustrating process for both of them, but Kevin's glowing smile at each tiny success made the effort worthwhile. When he printed the last of the words on his list perfectly, she hugged him.

"That's exactly right. I think you deserve a reward. What would you like?"

His eyes widened. "You mean like a present or something?"

She grinned at his look of delight. "A small present."

He chewed on his lip thoughtfully, then finally said, "I'm really hungry. Could I have a hamburger?"

It wasn't exactly what she'd had in mind, but he was looking at her so expectantly, she shrugged. "Why not? I'm sure we can find someplace nearby for a hamburger and maybe even some french fries."

"Great, but what about my dad?"

Liz wasn't much in the mood to talk to Todd Lewis about anything, but regulations demanded it. "If you give me the number, I'll call him at his office and get his okay."

Kevin's face fell. "He doesn't work in an office. You can't call him."

She should have realized that the minute she'd made the first call last week and gotten only an answering machine. "Where does he work?"

"He builds stuff. You know, like shopping centers and things. He's building one now that's really neat."

Liz made one of those impetuous decisions that occasionally got her into very hot water. She didn't believe in breaking rules, but she sometimes bent them in two if she thought it would help one of her students. Right now, Kevin needed all the positive reinforcement she could give him. She'd brave a lion in his den, if that's what it took. Todd Lewis seemed only slightly less formidable.

"Do you know where it is?"

"Sure. He takes me with him lots on the weekends. Sometimes we even go by at night, if he has to go back and work late."

It didn't sound like any sort of life-style for a young boy, Liz decided, and only added to her conviction that Todd Lewis was treading dangerously close to being an unfit father. Yet Kevin always spoke of his father with such obvious pride. He clearly idolized the man. That intrigued her.

"Come on, then," she said to Kevin. "Let's go see him."

When they found Todd Lewis, he was standing with one dusty, booted foot propped on a steel girder that was about to be hoisted to the third level of a future parking garage. A yellow hard hat covered much of his close-cropped brown hair and shaded his face. A light blue work shirt was stretched taut over wide shoulders. Liz found herself swallowing hard at the sight of him. He was bigger—at least six-foot-two and probably two-hundred pounds—more imposing and more masculine than she'd imagined. He made her feel petite and fragile and very much aware of her wrinkled shirt, the run in her hose and the fact that she hadn't stopped long enough to put on lipstick.

His eyes, when she got close enough to see them, sparked with intelligence and curiosity. At the sight of his son running toward him, those eyes filled with something else as well, a warmth and concern that startled her and made her wish for one wild and timeless moment that the look had been directed at her.

"Dad, this is Mrs. Gentry," Kevin blurted with a wave of his hand in her direction. Something in Todd Lewis's self-confident demeanor seemed shaken by that announcement, but there was no time to analyze it because Kevin was rushing on. "We came to see you because we're going to celebrate, but Miss Gentry said we had to get your permission and you don't have a phone here, so I showed her where you are. Is it okay?"

There was another flash of amazement in those clear hazel eyes. An errant dimple formed in that harsh, tanned face. "A celebration?"

"Yeah. I got all my homework right. Mrs. Gentry helped me while we were waiting for you. I told her you were coming, but that sometimes you got really busy and forgot things. You know like you did when you had that date last week and she came to the house all dressed up and you were working on the car."

Liz noted that Todd Lewis nearly choked at that. She figured the revelation served him right.

"Sorry," he said. "I told him to tell you I'd be there today or tomorrow."

He didn't sound the least bit repentant. Before she could stop herself, she reminded him, "And I asked you to come in today. I'm sure if you'd explained things to your boss, you could have arranged for the afternoon off."

"I am the boss," he said matter-of-factly. "And I can guarantee you that I didn't get the title by walking off the job in the midst of a crisis just because of some damned whim."

Liz had to do some quick revising. She glanced around at the sprawling mall with its Spanish-style architecture, man-made lakes and fountains already bubbling. Even weeks away from completion, it promised to be spectacular. How on earth could a man in charge of all this run a business without an office? Perhaps he was one of those laid-back eccentrics who delighted in going his own way and was talented enough or wealthy enough to get away with it. She, however, didn't operate that way.

"It was hardly a whim, Mr. Lewis. If I hadn't thought it extremely important, I wouldn't have requested the meeting."

"Demanded."

"Semantics, Mr. Lewis. The point is that you did not come. Again," she added.

"I'm sorry," he said again, this time sounding genuinely apologetic. "Your earlier notes..." He gazed pointedly at Kevin. "They seem to have gone astray."

She felt some of her tension and antagonism begin to ease. That put things in a slightly different light. She should have guessed that Kevin hadn't passed them along to his father.

"And the phone messages?"

He stared at her blankly. They both turned to gaze at Kevin. He was staring at his shoes.

"Sorry, Dad. I guess maybe they got erased."

Todd Lewis sighed wearily. "We will talk about all of this later, son." He smiled at Liz and shrugged. "I guess that explains that. I really am sorry. No wonder you had such a lousy impression of me."

Liz blushed as she thought of the barely veiled charges she'd leveled at him in her last note. She probably owed him an apology of some sort. Still, he had ignored that one. He wasn't entirely blameless. Or was he?

"You did get the note I sent yesterday, didn't you?"

"Yes."

"Well..." If she'd expected to intimidate Todd Lewis with a cool stare and an unyielding attitude, she'd vastly underestimated him. Those hazel eyes pierced her without once wavering.

"It is nearly five o'clock, Mr. Lewis," she stated pointedly, not sure why she felt the need to attack rather than be conciliatory. Perhaps it was because she wasn't one bit happy about the way her pulse had been skipping erratically ever since she'd gotten within five feet of Todd Lewis.

He grinned. Her pulse leapt. She wanted to attack. Yes, indeed, that was it. An instinctive and vitally necessary response.

"Thank you for enlightening me," he retorted. He held out his hand, displaying a forearm that was bare to the rolled-up sleeve of his shirt. "I don't wear a watch on the job. I don't like clock-watchers."

She wasn't sure whether he was referring to himself, his employees or her. Either way, if he'd hoped to rattle her, it was working. She couldn't take her eyes off that muscular forearm. If the man weren't quite so large or quite so masculine, she'd be tempted to grab it and experiment with that self-defense technique she'd learned at her last karate lesson. The prospect of flipping him onto his backside cheered her considerably.

"You know what I meant," she said stiffly. "I expected you at 3:30."

"And I had hoped to be there," he said so solemnly that she knew he was mocking her. "You know Miss Gentry..."

He made it sound as though she were some dried-up old prune. "*Mrs.* Gentry," she retorted.

He shrugged indifferently. That faint suggestion of amusement continued to play about his lips. "You may be in charge of your classroom, *Mrs.* Gentry, but I'm in charge around here. Unfortunately at a construction site things are apt to go wrong according to whim, rather than your rigid schedule. If you can think of some way to make these girders do your bidding, more power to you. I've had a helluva time with it."

This time he waited expectantly. Liz felt her insides quiver. Possibly with fury. More likely with something entirely less rational. The man was positively maddening. And far too attractive. She suspected the two characteristics were probably related. She realized she was gripping the handle on her purse so tightly the leather was biting into her flesh. She tried to relax. When that didn't work, she went for the jugular.

"You've already explained that you run the company, Mr. Lewis. You don't strike me as the sort of man who'd be foolish enough to believe he's either indispensable or indestructible. I'm sure you have assistants who could handle any crisis that occurs in the brief time it would have taken for you to keep an appointment with me.''

He simply scowled at the note of censure. ''That's not the way I do things,'' he said with finality. ''Now what was so all-fired important that it couldn't wait another twenty-four hours?''

She glanced at Kevin and hesitated. She'd already said far more than she should have in front of him. What on earth had gotten into her? ''I don't think this is the time or place to be discussing this.''

''You picked it,'' he reminded her.

''Mr. Lewis!''

He stared at her intently, then finally nodded. ''Kevin, go into the trailer and ask Hank if he'll take you to the top of the garage. It's another story higher since the last time you were here.''

''Oh, wow! Great, Dad. Thanks.'' He bounded off without a second glance at either of them.

Todd Lewis watched Kevin until the door of the construction trailer slammed behind him. Then once again he propped his foot on a pile of girders, put his elbow on his knee and said, ''You were saying...''

Liz sighed at the challenge and tried very hard not to stare at the way his jeans stretched across his hips. ''Mr. Lewis, I did not come here to argue with you. I came to ask permission for Kevin to have a hamburger with me as a reward for working so hard this afternoon.''

''Are you sure you didn't just want to check out his irresponsible father firsthand?''

The teasing glint in his eyes unnerved her. Again. "I'm sorry for some of the things I suggested in the note."

"But not all?"

"Kevin is a problem."

"Maybe you just don't know how to manage him."

The cool, unexpected taunt struck home. Liz practically shook with indignation. It was a welcome relief after all those other feelings she'd been experiencing.

"Don't you dare try to turn this into my failure, Mr. Lewis. Since you are so cognizant of your responsibilities, I'm surprised you don't pay more attention to Kevin. Surely he counts among them. If you had, you would have noticed long ago..."

Her furious tirade faltered as his expression suddenly became all hard angles. She'd seen pictures of cold, merciless dictators who looked less severe. His eyes glinted dangerously. She actually shivered as he took a long stride to tower over her. For an instant she regretted the impulsive tongue-lashing.

"I do know my son. He's a good kid. Maybe a little high spirited, but that's all to the good in a boy. Kevin and I do just fine," he said in a voice that chilled. "We don't need some high-minded do-gooder interfering in our lives. If he's having a problem with his schoolwork, we'll talk about it. Otherwise, you stay the hell out of our lives."

She flinched under the attack, then dared to glower right back at him. This was too important for her to back down now. "I can't do that. Kevin is in trouble in school and that's my responsibility."

"Fine. I said I was more than willing to talk about his schoolwork. I'll be there tomorrow afternoon, no matter what the damn girders do. Now, if you don't mind, I'll be getting back to work."

He strolled away without a backward glance. Before Liz could fully recover from the unnerving confrontation, she saw the burly, redheaded man who'd accompanied Kevin to the top of the skeletal structure join Todd Lewis. Hank, that was his name, she recalled as she watched them. For some reason, she couldn't tear her gaze away from the encounter between the two men. She couldn't shake the feeling that she was seeing a drama of some sort unfold. Suddenly, with a sinking sensation in the pit of her stomach, she realized that Kevin wasn't with them. Even from a distance, she thought she could see Todd Lewis's complexion turn ashen. He reached in his shirt pocket and drew out a pack of cigarettes. He shook one out, then replaced the pack. Oddly, he didn't light it. A minute later, he threw it down and ground it under his work boot. She recognized it at once as the nervous ritual of a reformed smoker.

Unaware that she had even begun to move, she found herself not more than a few feet away. She heard Todd Lewis's harsh oath and Hank's apology.

"I swear, Todd, I thought he was coming right back to you. You want me to get the men together?"

"Not yet. What exactly did he say?"

"He asked me for some quarters for the soda machine, then he took off. That's it. Last I saw him, he was in the trailer getting a drink. If he's not there and he's not with you, I don't know where the hell he could have gone."

Hesitantly, Liz touched Todd Lewis's arm. "You think he heard us arguing, don't you? You think he's run away."

He turned on her, his shoulders tense, his jaw tight. That furious stance might have frightened her, if she hadn't looked into his eyes. There was the expected flash of anger, but there was also panic and a touching vulnerability.

That glimpse into Todd Lewis's soul removed forever any lingering doubts she might have had about the depth of his love for his son. It also left her shaken in a way she couldn't begin to understand.

Chapter Two

Todd felt like strangling somebody. Right now it was a toss-up whether it should be Hank or Elizabeth Gentry. He glowered at both potential victims, then muttered a curse under his breath. There was no point in blaming them. They looked every bit as worried and dismayed as he felt. Besides, he was the guilty one. He knew how sensitive Kevin was, how easily hurt. He should never have been discussing him where Kevin might overhear the argument. The kid had a way of popping up when you least expected it. Sending him off with Hank had been no guarantee he wouldn't be back ten seconds later.

"Hank, you take your car and head east," he said finally, fighting to think clearly through the haze of self-recriminations. With great effort, he kept his voice calm and reasonable. "I'll go west on foot. He can't have gotten too far."

Hank, the most easygoing man he'd ever known, looked downright uncomfortable.

"What is it?" Todd demanded impatiently.

"Don't forget he had those quarters. He could have taken a bus."

The already tense muscles across Todd's shoulders knotted. Only the quiet presence of Elizabeth Gentry kept him from uttering a whole arsenal of swear words. He closed his eyes and imagined shouting every one of them at the top of his lungs. Even the imagery had a restorative effect.

"Okay," he said with the careful deliberation of a man battling hysteria. He clung to his businesslike ability to remain calm in a crisis, to put his emotions on hold until every last detail had been handled. "Then we'd better take both cars. We'll meet back here in an hour."

To his amazement he sounded decisive and controlled. He felt as though he were splintering apart.

"What about me?" a soft voice interrupted. "What can I do?"

Todd stared at her. "I think you've done enough for one afternoon," he said in a cutting tone that brought Hank's head snapping up. Elizabeth Gentry stared back at Todd. She appeared serene and unfazed by his bark, but there was fire in her eyes. That look challenged him to put aside his animosity for Kevin's sake or further establish her impression of him as a jerk.

"Oh, hell," he said finally. "Come with me."

"Wouldn't it be better if I took my own car? I'll drive south toward the school. He might have gone back that way."

"I think school's the last place he's likely to head," Todd retorted, wondering why the hell she'd bothered to ask his opinion, since she had every intention of doing exactly as she pleased.

Her cool demeanor slipped just a bit at his pointed sarcasm. Then her chin jutted up. "Fine. I'll go north. Let's just stop wasting time."

With that she stalked off, her head held high, her back as ramrod straight as he'd once imagined it to be. The effect, though, wasn't at all what he'd anticipated. Thoroughly bemused, he stared after her.

How had he gotten it so wrong? Kevin's teacher was no prim, dried-up Victorian maiden. Far from it. She was all ripe curves and passionate indignation. Even with his son missing and his anger fueled, he'd still had the most overpowering urge to tangle his fingers in that flame-red hair of hers and hush her with a bruising, breath-stealing kiss. Desire had slammed through him with the force of a hurricane sweeping across the Florida keys. Its unexpectedness had stunned him.

Her amber eyes had challenged him in a way that made his heart pound louder and faster than any jackhammer. Her derision had irked him. Her sensuality had provoked him. The hell of it was, she was also married. *Mrs. Gentry.* The combination was enough to set off warning bells so loud only a man stone deaf could ignore them. Elizabeth Gentry spelled trouble and it had very little to do with her threats about Kevin.

One good thing had come of the encounter: he knew with absolute certainty now that she would never turn her disagreement with him into a public squabble with the authorities. She'd only used the threats to assure Kevin's well-being. He'd seen the genuine concern and affection in her eyes, the caring that ran as deep and true as a mother's fierce protectiveness. It was a look that could make any man less wary than he fall in love. It was a look he couldn't ever recall seeing in Sarah's eyes, at least not toward the end.

With a disgusted shake of his head, he snapped his attention back to Kevin's disappearance. Still muttering apologies, Hank had already followed the teacher to the parking lot. Todd sprinted to his own mud-streaked, battle-scarred pickup. Gravel flew as he spun out onto Kendall Drive, forcing his way into the stream of rush-hour traffic. Locked into a slow-moving crawl, he kept his eyes peeled for some sign of a small, proud boy walking dejectedly along the edge of the highway.

His impatience mounted with every block. Horn honking, he tried weaving through traffic, but it was a wasted effort. No lane was moving any faster than a snail's pace. With each quarter mile he covered, his panic deepened. So many terrible things could happen to a kid, especially in a city the size of Miami. Kevin was all he had, all that meant anything in his life. If anything happened to him... He couldn't even allow himself to complete the thought.

His heart thudded heavily as dismay settled in. This was pointless. He'd already covered miles without seeing any sign of Kevin. If he had gotten on a bus, he could be anywhere. If he hadn't and if he'd come this way, Todd would have found him by now.

Praying that Hank or Elizabeth Gentry had had better luck, he finally turned the truck around and went back to the nearly deserted construction site. The crew, unaware that there had been any sort of a crisis, had left in his absence and only one car remained in the lot—hers. In an odd way it reminded him of her. It was an ordinary, small blue Toyota, sedate and practical. Only the sunroof hinted at her sense of daring.

Had she found Kevin, he wondered as he hurried toward the trailer. If she had, he thought he might be able to forgive her anything.

He swung open the door of the trailer and saw the two of them—laughing. Her laughter was low and full-bodied. Kevin's high-pitched and raucous. Her arm was around the boy's shoulders as they studied a drawing done in red marker. The quiet intimacy of the scene, the suggestion of family, made Todd suck in his breath. For an instant an irrational fury clouded his vision, overriding his relief. He'd been out searching, his stomach knotted by worry and they were in here laughing like two thoroughly happy conspirators.

"Where'd you find him?" he asked. His curt tone drew startled glances from both of them.

"Hi, Dad," Kevin said cheerfully, obviously oblivious to his father's mood. Todd regarded him suspiciously. He was not behaving like a child who'd run away in anger.

"We've been waiting for you. See what I did. Mrs. Gentry says it's pretty good."

A surge of righteous outrage burst inside him. "Go to the truck," he said, his voice tight.

"Dad?" Kevin's voice was puzzled, his expression confused. He stared up at his teacher, which only infuriated Todd more. Since when had Kevin turned to someone other than him for instructions.

"Now!"

Shoulders slumping and lip quivering at the shouted command, Kevin started toward the door.

"I think you'd better let me explain," Elizabeth Gentry said. She spoke quietly, but there was an edge of steel in her voice. He knew instinctively it was her classroom voice. It probably terrorized the kids. He ignored it.

"Kevin, you heard what I said." His voice was calmer, but no less authoritative.

She stepped closer to Kevin and put a protective hand on his shoulder. She glared defiantly at Todd, the look meant to put him in his place. He had to admire her spunk. Under less trying circumstances, he might even find it a turn-on. Right now, it was only an irritant. He scowled right back at her.

"Save your attempt at intimidation, Mr. Lewis. Kevin did not run away. Don't take your frustration out on him or, for that matter, on me."

He stared from her to his son and back again. Swallowing hard, he tried to regain control over his temper. "I don't understand."

"Tell your father what happened," she urged. When Kevin appeared to be hesitant, she smiled at him. "It's okay. Tell him what you told me."

"I went to get a drink. Hank gave me the money. And there was this cat." He regarded Todd hopefully. "It was a great cat, Dad, but he'd gotten all wet. I guess he fell in that big mud puddle in back of the trailer. Anyway, I tried to get him so I could clean him up, but he ran. I chased him across the field. When I came back, you were all gone. I must have been gone longer than I thought, 'cause Mrs. Gentry says you all were worried. I'm sorry I scared you."

Relief rushed through Todd. A cat! Kevin had been chasing a stupid, wet cat. He massaged his temples. The pounding in his head began to ease as his tension abated. He stared at Elizabeth Gentry and gave a small, apologetic shrug before grinning sheepishly at Kevin. "Did you catch the cat?"

"No," he said, obviously disgusted. "He was too fast. Anyway, he ran inside a garage. I guess he must belong to somebody."

Suddenly exuberant, Todd picked Kevin up and swung him in the air. "You want a cat that badly?"

"Not really. I'd rather have a dog, but you said we couldn't have one, 'cause we're not home enough." He recited Todd's old argument without emotion. "I just wanted to play with this one."

"Maybe we'll have to rethink that," Todd said. He caught Elizabeth Gentry watching them. She was smiling, but there was something about her eyes that got to him. She looked sad. He couldn't imagine why. Everything had turned out just fine. His son was safe. He felt like celebrating.

"I'd better be getting home," she said, the flat declaration tempering his mood.

Suddenly uncertain, he said with awkward sincerity, "Thanks for helping with the search."

"I'm glad it wasn't really necessary. I will see you at the school tomorrow, won't I?"

The woman had the tenacity of a terrier with an old sock. He grinned. "I promise not to stand you up again." He took her hand, holding it just long enough to confirm the solemnity of his commitment. Her grip was firm, her skin like cool silk, but she trembled. That tiny hint of vulnerability set off warning bells again. He released her hand, but not her gaze. The air sizzled with electricity.

"Hey, you guys, what about my hamburger?"

Todd glanced away at last to stare blankly at Kevin. When he looked back at Elizabeth Gentry, her cheeks were flushed, her eyes hooded.

"I don't think today is . . ." she began with surprising uncertainty.

Kevin's face fell. Todd was torn between his son's disappointment and his own need to escape the confusing emotions this redheaded firebrand raised in him.

"I'll take you out for a hamburger, son. Mrs. Gentry probably has to get home to her family."

"No, she doesn't. She doesn't have a family. She told us her husband died," Kevin announced ingenuously.

Todd's heart took an unexpected lurch. Glancing over Kevin's head, his eyes met hers. "I'm sorry."

"So am I," she said quietly, but with a surprising lack of emotion.

Todd felt guilty at the relief that swept through him. He had not wanted Elizabeth Gentry to have a husband. He was equally glad to see that it didn't appear she was living with ghosts, though why it mattered was beyond him. He didn't date women like the one standing before him. He ran like crazy from innocence and vulnerability and commitment.

"See, Dad, I told you," Kevin was saying. "Besides, she promised. She should come, too. She's probably really hungry by now."

Suddenly bolder, Todd surveyed her from head to toe with lazy deliberation, then felt renewed guilt at the look of confusion his teasing aroused. For some reason he wanted to provoke her into a mild flirtation. Perhaps he merely wanted to prove to himself that she was as unfeminine and boring as he'd once imagined her. Maybe he just wanted to shake her cool facade. Either way he knew he was playing with fire.

"Are you?" he asked in a voice thick with innuendo.

Startled eyes blinked at him. "What?"

"Hungry?"

As if she suddenly guessed the rules by which he was playing, she returned his impudent look with a touch of defiance. "Starved, actually."

Todd laughed at the prompt response to his challenge. "Then the two of you go on. I'll meet you there in a few minutes. I just want to finish up a little paperwork and wait for Hank to get back. If none of us is here, he'll worry himself to death."

"Dad, it's already late. Couldn't you just leave him a note?"

"It won't be long."

Kevin's forehead creased with a worried frown. "You won't forget or something, will you?"

The question told Liz all too much about his tendency to get caught up in work. He caught the quick flare of concern in her eyes. Todd's gaze locked with those serious amber eyes. "No," he promised softly. "I won't forget."

With an odd tightening in his chest, he watched the two of them walk away from the trailer. She bent down to listen to something Kevin was saying, then the two of them laughed, the happy sound rippling through the evening air. How long had it been since he'd shared laughter like that with a woman? He hadn't trusted any of them since Sarah. Something told him, though, that he could trust Elizabeth Gentry. He wondered if he'd have the courage to try.

Before he could immerse himself in wasted philosophical musings, Hank came back. He gazed after the departing woman, noting the child by her side, then directed a searching look at Todd.

"Everything okay?"

"Fine."

"Who's the looker?" The interested query was made with Hank's usual lack of tact and reflected his appreciation of all things feminine.

Todd bristled. "Kevin's teacher," he said stiffly, not sure why he felt so resentful of the innocently chauvinistic remark.

"Why didn't I ever have a teacher who looked like that?" Hank said wistfully. "I might have learned more."

"You have an engineering degree now. What more would you have learned?"

"Life, my friend. A woman like that could teach you all about life."

Todd groaned. "Does your libido ever take a rest?"

"Not since junior high," Hank retorted with an unrepentant grin.

"Go heft a few girders, then. Maybe it'll wear you out." He picked up a folder of papers and stuffed them in his briefcase.

"Not a chance. Let me know if you're not interested in that one. Maybe I'll take a shot at her. I have a real thing for redheads."

Todd looked up, incensed. "She's Kevin's teacher, dammit. Not some floozy you saw in a bar. Stay sway from her."

Hank stared at him consideringly. "So, then, you are interested."

Todd slammed his fist on the desk, scattering papers. "I am not interested. I am just trying to see that my son and I get through the school year without being responsible for his teacher's downfall."

His outburst didn't seem to faze Hank. "Don't worry about that," he said easily. "I'll absolve you of all responsibility. Just give me her name and I'll take it from there. I won't even mention I know you."

"Hank!"

"Yes, partner?"

Todd recognized that innocent tone all too well. He shook his head. "Take a hike, buddy."

"Right."

Todd heard him chuckling as he left the construction shed. One of these days a brave and daring woman was going to come along and capture Hank Riley's outrageously fickle heart. Todd just hoped he'd be around to watch the fireworks.

Less than an hour later Todd Lewis slid into the booth across from Liz, his long legs immediately and sensuously tangling with hers. He did it deliberately. She knew it. She sat up straighter and tried to draw away, but there was no way to escape, not when the man was dead set on rattling her. She recognized that perfectly innocent gleam in his eyes for exactly what it was. Temptation! A flat-out dare, which no lady would take and every woman dreams about.

Liz returned his gaze evenly, determined not to let him see that his touch was affecting her in the slightest, that it had been driving her crazy all afternoon long. Beneath the table, though, her fingernails were probably cutting right through the booth's bright blue plastic seat covers.

"Where's Kevin?" Todd asked, glancing around the crowded restaurant. Sound echoed off the glass walls and tiled floors. It was one of those places that had apparently been designed on the theory that the more noise there was in a restaurant, the more convinced people would be that they were having fun.

"He made a dash for one of the video games the minute we walked through the door."

"And you didn't dash with him?"

"I told him I'd order."

"After making such a fuss to get you to come, he shouldn't have left you alone. I'll go get him."

"Mr. Lewis—"

"Todd."

"*Mr. Lewis*, I'm used to being on my own. Kevin's with a friend. Let him enjoy himself. Besides, it would probably embarrass him to have anyone catch him with his teacher."

Her easy acceptance of being abandoned amazed him. A lot of women would have been insulted, even if the male who'd left them was only eight. "You really understand kids, don't you?"

"Don't sound so surprised. It is my job," she said, then added, "but if what you're really saying is that I genuinely seem to like kids, the answer is yes. I think they're great. They usually say exactly what's on their mind and they're open to new experiences."

"What about you? Are you open to new experiences?"

He was doing it again, lacing the conversation with enough innuendos to disconcert a saint. "I'd like to think so," she managed to say without stumbling over the response.

Todd settled back in the booth. "Then I think we should get to know each other better, don't you?"

"I suppose," she said cautiously, making the mistake of meeting his steady gaze. Her heart somersaulted. Those eyes of his could lure a woman into forgetting all reason, to say nothing of professional ethics and quite possibly her name. Her hands slid right off the seat. She clasped them tightly in her lap, drew in a shaky breath and added quickly, "For Kevin's sake."

He nodded. "Of course. Why don't we start by using first names?"

"I really don't think it would be appropriate, especially not in front of Kevin."

"But he's not here right now. Let's compromise. You call me Todd and I'll call you Miss Liz."

She grinned despite herself. "You call that a compromise?"

"You'd rather call me Mr. Todd?"

A faint smile playing about his lips mocked the seriousness of his tone. Liz frowned at his determined impudence, but she couldn't bring herself to look away. Retreat now would give him a victory in a battle she'd almost forgotten how to fight. Instead the tension built just as it had earlier, crackling through the air like summer's lightning.

It was Kevin who broke it, joining them with a huge grin on his face.

"Hey, Dad, guess what! I beat Joey Simons at Battle of the War Lords!"

"That's great, son," he said without taking his eyes from her mouth for one single second. Her lips were parched and she wanted very badly to run her tongue over them, but knew perfectly well that would only inflame the situation. She grabbed her glass of water and drank the whole thing. Todd grinned with unabashed satisfaction.

"Will you and Mrs. Gentry play with me?" Kevin pestered. "Joey had to go home."

With obvious reluctance, Todd tore his gaze away from her and looked at Kevin. "What about your hamburger? It should be here in a minute."

"Oh, yeah." He slid in next to his father. "I forgot."

Watching Kevin and his father together, Liz felt a lump lodge in her throat. Suddenly she wanted to cry. There was so much adoration in Kevin's eyes, such a sense of camaraderie between them, it almost reminded her of... Closing her eyes against the surge of pain, she sealed off the thought before it could form.

"I think I should be going," she said suddenly, just as the meal arrived. "I'll pay the check on my way out."

"No!" The protest was voiced by father and son.

"Really, it's late." She needed to escape before the threatening tears embarrassed her.

"We just got here. You haven't even eaten your hamburger," Kevin said.

"I'm not really hungry. Your father can have it."

"A little while ago you said you were starving," Todd reminded her. His penetrating gaze seemed to see right through her flimsy excuse.

"Besides, it won't be the same," Kevin said. "You promised me a celebration."

At the mention of the promise, her determination wavered. Kevin might be manipulating, but he was using the truth to do it. She had promised. However, if she'd had any idea what sitting in this booth across from Todd Lewis would be like, she would have devised some other reward for Kevin. She would have seen to it that it didn't require being crowded into such close quarters with a disturbingly masculine parent who insisted on toppling all barriers between them, starting with the informal way he meant to address her. *Miss Liz, indeed!*

Kevin was gazing at her now with wide, hopeful eyes. His father's eyes had a speculative gleam in them, as if he'd guessed that he was the reason for her desire to run and was wondering how to capitalize on his advantage. That decided her. She would stay. She would eat every bite of her hamburger, even if she choked on it.

She gave Todd Lewis her most defiant, go-to-hell glare and picked up the ketchup. Her gaze never wavered as she shook the bottle. Kevin's sharp gasp drew her attention. She glanced down. Her hamburger had virtually disappeared in a sea of thick red ketchup. She groaned. How could she have done something that stupid?

"I'll order you another one," Todd said, reaching for her plate.

She grabbed it back. "This one's fine. I like a lot of ketchup." Her tongue nearly tripped over the flat-out lie. Still, she refused to admit to her foolish mistake.

"Don't be ridiculous. I'll take it and get you another one."

"I'll just scrape a little of this off," she said stubbornly.

He shrugged finally. "Suit yourself."

Liz determinedly scraped off enough ketchup to serve all the fans at Joe Robbie Stadium during next Sunday's Dolphins game. She took her first bite, then forced a smile as Kevin and Todd watched her expectantly.

"You're sure it's okay?" Todd asked, his expression doubtful.

"Just fine," she said with forced cheer.

To herself, she vowed to get through the next half hour without coming unglued, if it was the last thing she ever did. She also swore that she would not under any circumstances ever admit to either of the males across from her that she absolutely never ate ketchup. It gave her hives.

Chapter Three

Todd pulled his pickup into the lot behind the elementary school. The dusty playground was empty, except for a forgotten soccer ball. The swings shifted slowly in the hot stirring of humid air. The cloudless sky burned a merciless reminder that Miami was still weeks away from the first cool nights and gentle days.

As if the weather weren't enough to sap energy, Todd felt an age-old feeling of intimidation squeezing his chest as he walked around the corner of the low, brick building. When he'd finally graduated from high school two years late, he'd vowed never to cross the threshold of another school. He was here now only because of Kevin. And one feisty teacher who wouldn't let well enough alone, he reminded himself.

As he neared the entrance, he heard the faint ringing of a bell and a moment later the quiet erupted into a scene of absolute chaos. Several hundred noisy, rambunctious students began pouring through the doors like salmon frantic to get upstream. He stood out of the way and watched, hoping to catch a glimpse of the determinedly staid Mrs. Gentry in the midst of the pandemonium.

It took him only a few minutes to spot her. Her red hair was pulled tautly back. Curly strands, indifferent to her efforts at restraint, had escaped to create a halo that glittered a coppery gold in the sunlight. In her slim beige skirt, emerald green silk blouse and sensible beige pumps, she was solemnly leading a perfectly formed line toward one of the bright yellow Dade County school buses. The impression of rigidity returned with a thud, correcting a night of more alluring dreams.

Then he saw a small girl of six or seven lift a laughing face toward her. Elizabeth's—Miss Liz's—generous mouth curved into an answering smile. With fingers that seemed somehow hesitant she reached out and lovingly brushed a strand of hair back from the child's face. There was an odd sense of yearning in that fleeting touch that wrapped itself around Todd's heart.

Contradictions! So many contradictions, he wondered if he'd ever understand them all.

There's a lifetime to try.

The unexpectedly wayward thought careened through his head, slamming into his consciousness with the impact of a fullback charging at full speed. His breath rushed out, followed by a colorful, resistant oath. There was no way in hell this woman—any woman—was going to get to him again. Not after Sarah.

But his palms were sweating like a lovestruck teen's and his heartbeat skittered and danced in a way he'd all but forgotten. He seized on past hurts and entrenched bitterness to chase away the symptoms of an imagination gone awry. They did a damn poor job of it, he noted wryly as he waited at the entrance for Elizabeth Gentry to join him. He rubbed his palms on his denim-clad thighs and hoped the heat in his loins would cool.

While he waited, she stood watching—a lone sentry—until the last school bus pulled away. Again he caught that flash of yearning on her face, the subtle droop of her shoulders when the children were out of sight. An aching need built in his chest, a need that made no sense. A tender wondering filled his soul with questions he wanted to ask, but didn't know how, didn't even know if he had the right to ask. Worse, he couldn't even imagine where all these thoughts were coming from. He covered his confusion with a smile meant to tease away the frown on her lovely face.

"Why so glum?" he asked softly, stepping from the shadows as she neared the front door.

Startled eyes met his. He thought there was the beginning of a smile, but it ended before it could brighten her face. She merely nodded in satisfaction.

"So, you came."

"I told you I would. Right on time, too," he noted as if seeking approval.

That did earn a full-blown grin. "Are you expecting a gold star for attendance? If so, it will hardly make up for all those zeros."

Despite her teasing tone, his voice and his mood went flat. "I stopped worrying about report cards long ago."

"Even Kevin's?" she queried briskly, chasing away any last remnants of the light mood.

Disappointed and unable to figure out why, he snapped, "You're all business, aren't you, Miss Liz?"

She scowled disapprovingly. The prim set of her mouth wasn't all that far removed from his original image of her. With an urge of pure devilment, he felt like kissing those lips until they were bruised and swollen and parted on a sigh of pleasure.

"It's Mrs. Gentry," she corrected with that familiar snap in her voice. "And I do try to act like a professional when I'm having a business meeting. Shall we go inside?"

"By all means," he said, responding to her cool demeanor with a touch of sarcasm he couldn't have stopped if he'd wanted to. The woman infuriated him. Worse, something told him she enjoyed it, that she liked watching the barriers go up. He wondered why. Did she need them there to protect her heart? Not from him. He wasn't interested. Perhaps he should tell her that.

As soon as they reached room one-twenty-two, she grabbed an eraser and attacked the blackboard as if the day's lessons had offended her by lingering on display. Chalk dust filled the air with a fine mist and a scent that dragged Todd back nearly twenty years.

He pulled a too-small chair up beside her desk, turned it around and sat down straddling it to wait. With each moment that passed, his impatience grew. Only when the blackboard was cleaned to her satisfaction and the chalk lined up neatly and the papers on her desk straightened into tidy piles, did she sit down. It took several more minutes for her to lift her gaze to meet his. Only then did he realize that she'd been gathering her composure, not putting him in his place.

"Tell me about Kevin," she suggested, idly scratching at a blotchy red spot on her arm. When she pushed up her sleeve, he saw the marks went all the way up.

"Are you okay?" he asked.

She regarded him blankly. He reached over and touched one of the raised blotches. "What happened?"

Red flamed her cheeks. "Hives," she said curtly. "About Kevin..."

Hives, hmm? Generally caused by allergies or nerves. He wondered which had caused hers? He decided not to ask. It would give him something to speculate about later, when her image was plaguing him.

"I thought *you* wanted to tell *me* about Kevin," he said instead. "Isn't that why we're meeting?"

"We'll get to my observations. I thought it might be helpful if I knew whether his behavior in school reflected his behavior at home. Does he give you any discipline problems?''

Sarah's complaints sprang to mind, but he shook his head. ''No more than any kid his age.''

She seemed surprised by that. ''Are you sure?''

''I know what I was like at Kevin's age. He's no different.''

She smiled. The effect was like the sun emerging on a cloudy day. It warmed his heart, even as she said, ''But I suspect you were a holy terror. That's hardly a fair comparison.''

''I turned out okay,'' he countered, responding to her amusement. ''For a holy terror, that is.''

''Don't you want more for Kevin?''

He sighed. ''I assume you're thinking ahead to college.''

She shook her head. ''Right now, I'm thinking ahead to passing third grade. He won't at the rate he's going.''

Her somber prediction had the desired effect. It shook him up as none of her vague warnings had. ''It's that bad?'' he said skeptically. ''Surely—''

''Mr. Lewis, he can't read.''

''He struggles over a few words.''

''The simplest words.''

''Then why did he pass second grade?''

''I can't account for another teacher's decision. All I can tell you is that the situation cannot continue without doing irreparable harm. Once a child has lost the chance to acquire solid reading skills, everything else becomes almost impossible. History, geography, science, even math. Kevin is bright, but he's frustrated and angry. He takes it out on his classmates.''

The scenario had an all-too-familiar ring to it. "Boys like to fight," he said defensively. "It's perfectly normal.''

"He's clobbered two girls in the last week," she said bluntly.

Todd was genuinely shocked at that. He found he could no longer cling to the hope that this was all a tempest in a teapot. He'd scattered blame and defenses since the conversation began and Liz had countered every one of them. "I'll see that he's punished.''

"I've already seen to that. More punishment is not the answer.''

"What then?''

"Testing. Maybe special classes.''

Todd felt his stomach knot. "I will not have my son made out to be different.''

"But he is different," she said with surprising gentleness. "Denying it won't help him.''

"Dammit, he's just a little boy," he snapped, frustration and anger on Kevin's behalf making his head pound. So much about this was familiar. Familiar and painful. He closed his eyes against Elizabeth Gentry's patient, compassionate expression. He rubbed his temples, but the throbbing kept on.

He loved Kevin, just the way he was. Why hadn't Sarah? Why couldn't Liz Gentry? He didn't expect him to scale intellectual mountains. He just wanted him to grow into a man who could take pride in whatever skills he had. His unquestioning love and support should be enough. It was more than he'd ever had. He had no idea how to explain all of that to the woman who was waiting so quietly for him to reach the right decision. Whatever the hell that was.

He studied her, wondering what made her tick, why she fought so hard for one little boy when there were dozens more needing her attention. Far more about her puzzled him. When had a woman so full of feminine promise become so wary around men, so determined to keep the focus of her life on her classroom? Or did he have that wrong, as well? Perhaps he was the only man who seemed to throw her.

"Why are you so uptight around me?" he asked suddenly.

She paled and said staunchly, "I am not uptight."

"Oh, really? Do you always destroy paper clips that way?"

"What way?" she said, staring at him blankly.

Liz recognized a desperate attempt at distraction when she saw one. Unfortunately, though, Todd Lewis was right. He was pointing toward her desk, smirking in satisfaction, mischief making his eyes sparkle. She glanced down. There was indeed a pile of twisted bits of metal in front of her. She sighed. Okay, so she was uptight. It didn't mean anything. Admittedly, though, it was usually the parents who got nervous about these conferences.

She took a closer look at Todd Lewis. He did not seem nervous. In fact, he looked every bit as overwhelming and lazily self-confident as he had the previous afternoon on his own turf. He'd obviously gone home to change before the meeting. His jeans were pressed. His shirt was crisply starched and open at the throat to reveal a tantalizing swirl of dark brown hair. His hair was damp and recently combed. He smelled of soap and the faintest trace of after-shave. It all added up to raw masculine appeal. Not even the fact that he was sitting on a scaled-down chair meant for third-graders diminished him. If anything, it simply emphasized his powerful build.

"I'll ask you again," he said. "Why do I make you nervous?"

"You don't make me nervous, Mr. Lewis." These flat-out lies were getting to be a habit around him. She scratched harder at her hives. "You make me mad." That, at least, was the truth.

It also made him tense up. "Meaning?"

"You and I seem to agree on one thing, that Kevin is a bright child. His IQ scores are well within the normal range, at the high end of the scale, as a matter of fact. Despite that, he is failing in school. His behavior is deplorable. In the last week he has bitten one classmate and bloodied the lip of another one. Is that the way you're rearing your son to respect girls?"

His distress seemed genuine. "I wish I had known about this sooner. Why didn't . . ."

"Don't even think about finishing that sentence. When was I supposed to tell you? When it first started happening? I wrote you a note after the first incident. I wrote you again after the second and third. You know that. You also know that my phone messages were intercepted."

"Which should tell you that Kevin knew exactly how upset I'd be. I don't tolerate that kind of behavior."

"Kevin's behavior is not the real problem."

"But you just said . . ."

"It's a symptom of his frustration. His self-esteem crumbles more each day that he can't keep up. From what I've observed and what little testing I am competent to do, I would guess that he has a learning disability. I think if you'd agree to testing, we could identify the problem and get Kevin the help he needs. Right now, he needs some positive things to start happening for him. Without the right kind of motivation, he'll just give up."

"Look, I love my son. I want him to have the best of everything, but I won't baby him," he said with that stubborn jut of his chin that was so often mirrored on Kevin's face. "He just needs to try harder. I'll have a talk with him."

Liz could see she wasn't getting through to him. "In Kevin's case, it's going to take more than talk. Please, let me have him tested."

"You said he needs the proper motivation. I'll see that he gets that."

There was an edge to his voice that told her exactly what Todd would consider proper motivation. Liz's heart sank.

"Why are you being so ridiculously stubborn about this? Your son's entire future may be at stake and you're acting as though it's a personal insult to suggest he have help.''

''Maybe that's it,'' he retorted unreasonably. ''Maybe I don't see where you get off telling me how to raise my son. You can't even keep your classroom under control. These fights are happening while he's under your supervision.''

''I can't prevent your son's disruptions unless I put him in a straightjacket,'' she reminded him tightly. ''I could suspend him. Is that what you'd prefer? That would take care of my problem, but it would do nothing about Kevin's.''

''I've told you I'll take care of that.''

''How? By punishing him? Pressuring him with expectations he can't possibly meet? How exactly do you plan to take care of it, Mr. Lewis? Are you capable of teaching him yourself? From what Kevin has told me, you don't even help him with his homework.''

He stood up. For a moment she had forgotten how tall he was, how impressively built. She felt her heart catch as he towered over her, his expression cold and unyielding.

''And that's *my* problem, isn't it? He's my son. What's the old saying about teachers? Those who can, do. Those who can't, teach. That's why you're in the classroom, isn't it? You don't know the first thing about raising a child of your own. You've never had to stay up through the night worrying whether a cough would turn into pneumonia or how you could make up for some terrible hurt. I spend every day of my life trying to make up to that boy for the mother he lost, the mother who didn't want him, didn't want either of us. I won't have him thinking that I don't believe in him."

Liz felt the sharp sting of tears. For an instant she wasn't sure if they were for Kevin and Todd Lewis or for herself. How dare he talk to her of loss as if she'd never experienced one of her own! How dare he suggest that she knew nothing of mothering and worrying and loving!

"You don't know what you're talking about, Mr. Lewis," she said coldly. She tried to tell herself that he was angry, that he was only lashing out because of what he perceived as an attack on his child. Still, the cruel comments hurt.

"I think I do know exactly what I'm talking about. I was wrong about you yesterday when I said you understood kids. You don't know the first thing about real kids and their needs. You learned it all in some textbook, but when it comes to kids who don't conform, who fight and get dirty and make mistakes, you can't handle it."

A memory, as sweet and clear as it was painful, skittered through her mind. Laura looking angelic in her new Easter dress. Then, moments later, the bow in her golden hair askew, a smile of delight on her face—and chocolate streaked from head to toe.

Todd's accusation was true. She had yelled at Laura over a silly dress. She had been upset. And it had all been over nothing. Today she would give anything to take back the words. She would barter with the devil himself to hold her child one more time, to feel those plump little arms around her neck, to kiss that choc-olate-sticky cheek.

She lifted eyes that shimmered with tears to stare at Todd Lewis. In a voice that shook with fury and an-guish, she said, "Don't patronize me, Mr. Lewis. I know exactly how hard it is to be a parent."

The words lingered in a moment of stunned silence before he said slowly, "You have a child?"

He sounded as if the very thought of it were mind-boggling. If she hadn't been hurting so at the flood of memories, she might have smiled at his startled expression. Instead, she simply shook her head.

"But Kevin said—"

"I *had* a child. She died when she was three. My husband died in the same accident. So don't tell me about loss, Mr. Lewis. Or guilt. Or worrying. Or lov-ing. I could write the textbook on every one of those emotions myself."

Chapter Four

If Liz's quietly spoken words stunned Todd, the stricken expression on her face was almost his undoing. She reminded him of a wounded doe. Her eyes turned bleak as her anger faded. As he watched, shadows of fear and dismay dimmed the sparkling amber to a dull, lifeless brown. He felt her loss as sharply as he'd once felt his own, recalling in vivid detail the emptiness of those painful weeks and months after Sarah had walked out of his life, the awful sense of betrayal, the hurt of rejection.

But he'd had Kevin and, oblivious to his father's grief and anger, four-year-old Kevin had filled the house with laughter and tears and impatient demands. For the last four years Kevin alone had kept the memory of love alive in Todd's aching, embittered heart. Kevin had been the one thing left worth fighting for. That much had never changed. He would still fight tenaciously for his son.

Liz had lost both husband and child. Todd couldn't imagine anything to compare with that.

"I'm sorry," he said softly, wishing he knew more comforting words. For the first time in many years he cursed the inadequacies that had kept his vocabulary unpolished, his manner rough. He knew all the right words to keep a crew of a hundred or more men in line and on schedule. He knew just what to say to difficult suppliers or demanding tenants. He even knew the glib and easy words necessary for a casual seduction. But in the presence of this kind and wounded lady, he knew a fierce longing to be a truly gentle man with a gift for mending.

He doubted, though, if she even heard the simple expression of regret. She seemed to be lost in some faraway place where no one could reach her. A single tear slid down her cheek. She didn't seem to notice that, either, but his insides twisted at the sight. A woman's tears had never affected him so before. Sarah had cried often and loudly, using tears as a weapon. He thought he'd become immune. But not now.

With a tenderness of which he'd always thought himself incapable, he reached over to brush that lone tear away. To his astonishment, his calloused fingers trembled as they encountered silken warmth. Another tear slid down to join the first, pooling against his fingertips.

"Don't cry," he pleaded, kneeling down beside her. The tears flowed more rapidly than ever, leaving her cheeks damp and his fingers helpless. He bit back an instinctive oath and said instead, "Please."

She looked at him then. She swallowed hard and blinked against the flood of tears, but the raw emotions held her captive. He saw the flare of determination in her eyes, the desperate appeal. Then he heard the tiny sigh of resignation as she wept on, as if the tears had been a long time coming and could no longer be denied.

Todd prided himself on being cool and distant and controlled. He'd hardened his heart against women when Sarah had said goodbye and no one since had come close to melting his icy reserve. Until this moment. Until tears had spilled down Liz Gentry's cheeks. Now he found to his amazement that his heart ached for her, wrenched by the awful loss that had bruised her very soul. He wasn't wild about the circumstances, but he was as helpless to turn his back on her as she was to cease the crying.

With a ragged sigh of his own, he gathered her to him. Settling awkwardly on the classroom floor, he was unmindful of the surroundings or their earlier, hateful exchange. He cradled her as he might have a brokenhearted child. It was an instinctive response to her need. Ironically, he found that it answered a pull deep inside him, as well; a yearning to protect and cherish that he'd felt for no woman since the early days with Sarah.

The sensation troubled him, but no more than the wild urgency of desire that zinged through him at the feel of her body in his arms. Yesterday's flash of hunger had been little more than a prelude to this. Her elusive, flowery scent fired his senses. Her fragility took him by surprise, reminding him in some purely primitive way of his own power and masculinity. She fit snugly against him, her reluctant arms held stiffly at her sides. He stroked and soothed, until her shoulders relaxed and her head rested against his chest. As her tears dampened his shirt, he murmured nonsensically, his voice low and tender. The scene was all wrong. It felt incredibly right.

He inflamed her. Innocently, unexpectedly, he set her skin on fire and turned the rhythm of his pulse to something hard and swift and dangerous.

Guilt swept through him, accompanying the passion. He hadn't meant for his touch to become anything more than a gesture of comfort and compassion, but he knew the instant that she responded, the second that his own muscles went taunt. Too many nights of longing and too many years of loneliness had crept up on both of them. Her pink lips parted on a startled sigh, the hand that had rested lightly against his chest moved restlessly, halting when fingertips touched the heated column of his neck. God, how he wanted her! How he wanted that tentative touch to explore and burn across his flesh! His body throbbed with the wanting.

It was the look of bewildered confusion in her eyes that stopped him. He struggled to match the overwhelming power of their unexpectedly unleashed desire with something more rational, something they wouldn't regret. He cupped her face in his hands and gently kissed away the last traces of tears. Anxious eyes watched him ... and waited, wanting, it seemed, what he wanted.

It took every ounce of control he possessed to move away. It took every last bit of strength to quiet his uneven breathing, to meet her gaze steadily as he lifted her back to her chair, settled her there and with a last tender touch let her go.

His arms felt empty. So damned empty. The sensation was oddly reassuring. It reminded him and perhaps even her that life went on. He knew then that he would not apologize. He would not pretend to regret the first honest emotion he had shared with anyone in years. Not normally one to analyze, he preferred to act. His withdrawal had caught him as much by surprise as had the desperate need he'd felt to have this woman. They were on a course that was unfamiliar to him. For the moment he left it to her to show the way.

"What do you want me to do?" he asked softly.

"Do?" she repeated, her expression puzzled. Her lower lip trembled and he wanted badly to still it with the touch of his own lips, to taste the salt of the tears that glazed her cheeks with a lingering dampness.

"About Kevin."

"Oh. Of course."

Her face, softened by the crying, carefully assumed its professional mask. Her voice, hoarse from weeping, turned crisp once more. Todd regretted that, as he hadn't regretted the rest of what had happened so spontaneously between them. Still, he turned away and paced, staring blankly out the windows, touching the pots of geraniums that dotted the sills with scarlet. His gift was no longer comfort but time. He gave her time to gather her composure around her like the protective cloak it was. His own emotions were in turmoil.

"I'm sorry," she said quietly into the stillness.

Frowning, he whirled on her, his own blood still pounding insistently. "Don't you dare be sorry," he said. His anger only seemed to dismay her more. He tried to gentle his tone, soften his fierce expression. "You . . . we have nothing to apologize for."

"I do. I should have stopped you."

"Nothing happened, dammit. You were upset. I tried to offer a little comfort."

"Oh, really?" Her half-formed smile bore a touch of cynicism. "It's gallant of you to put it that way, but we both know what really happened, what we almost did, and it would have been terribly wrong."

"Why?"

"You're Kevin's father. I'm his teacher."

"You're a woman first."

"Not here," she said stubbornly.

Todd sighed and shrugged helplessly. He knew when he was beat. For now. "There's no point in arguing with you when you get that high-minded note in your voice. You sound like a schoolmarm a hundred years ago, when some cowboy dared to steal a kiss."

Her face flamed with embarrassed color. "The rules haven't changed all that much," she said stiffly.

He wanted to shake her until she admitted that what had nearly happened between them had felt right, had felt good. Dear God in Heaven, he hadn't thrown her to the floor and made passionate love to her, though that's what he had wanted to do. Even now, he wanted to kiss the protests from her lips. He moved toward her. Her eyes widened. At her look of near-panic, he muttered a harsh curse under his breath and turned back toward the windows.

"We'll just pretend it never happened," she said hopefully.

"*It* never did," he said with wry amusement.

"You know what I mean."

"I don't think so," he said softly. He turned around and smiled. "Until the next time..."

She stared at him, shocked.

"There will be a next time," he insisted. "And until then, I want to remember every delightful minute of holding you in my arms. Besides, I've never been any good at make-believe."

She appeared crestfallen by his refusal to cooperate, by the blatant taunt in his voice. He felt a momentary pang of guilt for continuing to bait her, when he knew perfectly well that flirtation was as alien to her nature as it was natural to his. Yet he would not allow her to hide from the truth, to dismiss that spark of desire as if it had never existed. He'd felt alive again this afternoon and, by God, he wouldn't change a minute of it.

She drew herself up, her chin lifting to a proud angle. "Then perhaps you should consider transferring Kevin to another class."

"Not on your life," he said, suddenly furious. "This is between you and me. We're adults. We'll handle it. I will not allow it to affect my son."

"Mr. Lewis."

"Dammit, it's Todd. Say it." He bit out the rough demand, taking a step closer. Tight-lipped, she glowered at him. He waited.

"Todd," she whispered finally, but she wouldn't look at him when she said it.

He hadn't realized he'd been holding his breath, until it whooshed from him. He waited until she glanced up, then said, "Thank you."

She nodded. Cool. Distant. Controlled. It infuriated him.

"About Kevin," she prodded, clearly determined to get back on safer footing.

Unwilling to yield to a less personal exchange just yet, he held her gaze, trying to coax back the dangerous flare of intimacy. At last he recognized that the barriers were back in place to stay. He sighed wearily. "What do you want me to do?"

"There's a program," she began. The catch in her voice gave away her uncertainty. There was still a tiny chink in the wall. If he'd breached it once, he could do it again. If he dared. If he didn't care a whit about the consequences. If he could figure out exactly why it seemed to matter so much.

She took a deep breath and went on more firmly. "There's a really good psychologist in the Keys. She works with dolphins."

Despite everything, he found himself grinning, the hard knot in his belly dissolving as he came back to straddle the pint-sized chair beside her. "Dolphins? They need shrinks?"

To his delight, she smiled back, albeit a bit tremulously. "They do say they're almost human."

"Okay, I'll take your word for it. What about this psychologist?"

"Ann Davies. She's a good friend of mine. I'd like to have her test Kevin. Then she could recommend the next step. Maybe he'd even be qualified to be part of her program. It really is wonderful. It's innovative. If she'll take him, I just know she could help Kevin."

She sounded so hopeful, but even the prospect of testing daunted him. He seized on the one objection that seemed safe, the one possibility of preventing this whole useless process that raised hopes only to send them crashing against reality. "Are you suggesting that I send Kevin down to the Keys to live?"

"Of course not. He'd just go once a week."

"That's a long trek to manage every week. Who would take him?"

"If it turns out that's what's best for him, you would." She left him no room to argue about the inconvenience. She met his stubborn gaze with an unyielding tilt of her chin. Gone was any hint of vulnerability. The impassioned firebrand was back.

"Oh, for crying out loud," he muttered in disgust, but he knew he'd give in. He had a feeling in the end he'd find it impossible to deny this woman anything. It wasn't a realization he was crazy about.

"Just go down and talk to Ann," she urged, those wide, amber eyes beguiling him. It was like looking into the lure of whiskey and sensing salvation. It was probably twice as dangerous.

"If you're not comfortable with her and what she does, then I'm sure she can recommend someone here in Miami. Please."

He wasn't sure if it was the half-whispered plea or the eyes that implored that got to him, but he sighed heavily and surrendered. "Set it up."

Liz started calling her friend at six, while the memory of Todd Lewis's embrace still singed her memory. At first she had been horrified at breaking down the way she had. Then she realized that he hadn't been embarrassed, that he had reached out to her openly, easily. It told her a lot about his sensitivity and character, characteristics she might never have guessed at after seeing only his hotheaded stubbornness.

She also confessed to herself that she had liked being held in his arms, that she had wanted far more than she'd dared to admit to him. But it wouldn't happen again. She would not be caught alone with him again, not when they apparently set off enough sparks between them to rival the Fourth of July fireworks at Bayside.

It will not happen again, she thought firmly. It will not.

It will.

Oh, brother. She really needed to talk to Ann. Now. Tonight. And Kevin Lewis's problems, she finally admitted to herself, were the least of it.

She called every fifteen minutes, rejoicing when a busy signal finally replaced the unanswered ringing. When she finally got through at nine, Ann sounded cheerful but harried. Kids were arguing at the top of their lungs in the background. One seemed to be whimpering directly into Liz's ear. Probably the two-year-old. Melissa. Or was it Karen? She'd long ago given up trying to keep them straight. Besides, every time she turned around Ann was adding another one. Once in a while one of the foster kids was adopted by another family and Ann just turned right around and filled the empty bed. Her extended family grew and changed so rapidly, Liz wondered how she kept track without a scorecard and photographs posted on the oversized, industrial refrigerator that dominated the always busy kitchen.

"Pipe down, you guys," Ann bellowed, almost popping Liz's eardrum. Immediate silence descended.

"How do you do that?" Liz inquired with a familiar touch of awe.

"Don't give me that. I've been in your classroom. You're perfectly capable of achieving the same effect without even raising your voice."

"Some days I think I'd feel better, though, if I could just blast away. Doesn't it relieve the tension?"

"No. It only makes you hoarse, at least when you have to do it as often as I do around here. Jeremy, come take Melissa and put her to bed."

Melissa let out a wail of protest.

"Go," Ann said insistently. "I'll be in in a few minutes to kiss you goodnight. If you're not in bed with your face scrubbed and your teeth brushed, you won't get any ice cream for the next week."

The whimpers faded away.

"There now," Ann said. "That should give me a few minutes of peace and quiet. What's up?"

"A problem, as always."

"Hey, they're my speciality."

"I know but I tend to abuse the privilege."

"Not a chance. What's this one about? That pig-headed ex-mother-in-law of yours still giving you problems?"

"No," she said and hesitated. When she began again, it wasn't Todd she talked about. "It's one of my students." She detailed Kevin's behavior. "My guess is that he's dyslexic and that that's what's behind the hyperactivity. I also sense that he's heading for depression, if he doesn't see some improvement soon."

Ann chuckled. "Who gave you a license to practice all that psychological stuff?"

"Sorry. Just guesswork."

"Informed guesswork, my friend. I was only teasing. If you and Ed hadn't gotten married, you'd have gotten that Ph.D. and hung out your own shingle. It's still not too late for you to do it.''

''Ann . . .''

''Never mind, I won't press. So what do you want me to do about Kevin? Test him? You could have someone in Miami do that. I can give you names.''

''I know that, but I think this case needs your touch. The father is . . .'' She hesitated.

''Ohhh, I see,'' Ann said at once, her inflection wry. ''Just how difficult is he?''

The intuitive description was apt, but incomplete. ''He's not difficult exactly. He's just worried.''

''And resistant and mule-headed. What about the mother?''

''None on the scene. I'm not sure why.''

''Does that have anything to do with your special interest in the case? Is this fellow attractive in the bargain?''

''I hadn't noticed.''

Ann bellowed. ''Then they might as well bury you now and be done with it.''

''Okay, he is handsome,'' she admitted, knowing full well that the description was like calling the Eiffel Tower a cute little monument.

''I knew it. Sexy, too?''

There was the opening she'd been waiting for. Ann would listen. She wouldn't make judgments. She would give solid, no-nonsense advice. Liz decided that wasn't what she wanted right now, after all. She wanted to bask in the memories just a little longer, even if they were accompanied by a whole whirlwind of confusing thoughts and rampaging doubts.

"That is hardly the point," she said. "It's Kevin I'm worried about."

Ann backed off at once, but probably not for long. "Okay, bring your handsome-but-who-cares man down here and I'll work my wiles on him."

Liz hadn't counted on having to make the trip herself. "I wasn't going to come along," she protested. "I thought I'd just send him."

"Coward. Besides, if he's as unhappy about this whole idea as you say he is, he'll probably never get below Key Largo. That's where they usually chicken out. They stop for breakfast and by the time they're done, they've decided the whole trip is a waste of time. It's a long drive. They figure I really won't be able to help, anyway. The kid's complaining. He'd rather be playing baseball. Nope," she said emphatically. "I think you'd better come along."

"Okay," Liz said, laughing, ecstatic when she knew darn well she ought to be terrified. A whole day with Todd Lewis? She ought to have her head examined. "You've made your point. When?"

"Make it Saturday morning at eleven. I should be able to get this brood under control by then and meet you at my trailer at Dolphin Reach. If I'm not there, go visit Alexis. She's very pregnant and feeling put out because she doesn't think we're giving her enough attention."

"You are talking about a dolphin. What makes you think she's feeling put out?" Liz said.

"Because the fat rascal knocked me off the dock the other day, then skittered off on her tail fin. I swear she was laughing. I know the kids were."

"I'm sorry I missed the show."

"Hey, I suppose it was worth it. The man who was here to check out the center for a research grant thought the whole thing was so hilarious he approved the grant on the spot. It'll keep me in business another six months, anyway."

"Dammit, Ann, when are you going to start charging for what you do there?"

"I do charge," she said. "When the family can afford to pay."

It was an old argument and one Liz knew she had little chance of winning. Ann's soft heart would always win out over her business sense. "Well, just remember that Todd Lewis can afford it. In fact, if the price tag is high enough, he may actually take it seriously."

"You are getting devious, my friend."

"I wasn't until I met Todd Lewis," she said ruefully.

"Well, well," Ann said softly. "I thought I detected an undercurrent there."

Liz didn't like that knowing tone one bit. "Don't try to make something out of that," she warned.

The threat fell on deaf ears. "Honey, from the sound of it, I'm not the one who's in trouble here. I can't wait to meet your Mr. Lewis."

"He is not mine!" Liz bellowed.

She heard a hoot of laughter, then a soft click. She glared at the phone. How had she ever remained such good friends with such a know-it-all psychologist?

Chapter Five

Following the unanticipated Friday night arrival of a fast-moving cold front, the whole world had a surreal quality about it on Saturday morning. As Liz and Todd sped south on U.S. 1, the narrow ribbon of pavement seemed to disappear in a soupy morning mist. Cozy in the warmth of Todd's surprisingly utilitarian station wagon, it was as if they were alone on a shadowy planet.

"Whenever it's foggy like this, I always think of one of my favorite poems," she said as she stared dreamily out the window.

"'Fog.' Carl Sandburg," Todd said at once.

"Amazing. You know it?" She pulled her gaze from the fog-shrouded scenery to look at the man sitting beside her.

His lips curved sardonically at her obvious surprise. He recited the brief poem, then added, "They did teach poetry when I was in school."

"Sorry."

"Besides, I had a mother who thought every day should begin and end with Robert Frost or Emily Dickinson with an occasional diversion from one of the Brownings. Once you got beyond the one about fog, though, Sandburg was a little racy for her taste. 'Chicago' gave her palpitations."

"Naturally, that made you rush right out to read it."

His gaze slid away. "Nope," he said, concentrating on the highway. "I just took her word for it."

Increasingly curious, she prodded, "Then what is your taste in poetry?"

"Give me Bob Dylan any day."

She shot an amused glance at him. "I've never thought of Dylan as a poet."

"What are songs, if not poetry set to music?" A glint of mischief lit his eyes and her breath automatically caught in her throat. "Take 'Lay, Lady, Lay.' Now that is a great song. I've had a thing about brass beds ever since I first heard that song."

Liz ignored the innuendo and decided Todd Lewis would never know about the antique brass bed that she'd lovingly restored and now slept in. "I'm partial to 'Blowin' in the Wind' myself," she told him. "If pressed, though, I could probably make a case for 'Rainy Day Woman.'"

"Well, well, you are filled with surprises."

"As are you, Mr. Lewis."

"Todd," he coaxed, his quick glance beguiling. "Just for today, at least."

Lord, the man was persistent. She hadn't forgotten for one minute the whispered demand he'd made in her classroom and her own reluctant yielding. For some reason Todd Lewis was determined to manipulate their relationship into something personal. It had started even before he'd held her in his arms. Once they'd gotten past their initial antagonism over what was best for Kevin, he'd flirted outrageously. She was unaccustomed to such provocative teasing, but she knew enough not to think for one minute that it meant anything. Even without the benefit of Ann's usually sensible advice, she'd known enough to lecture herself repeatedly on that subject the last couple of days.

Besides, she'd told herself staunchly, the last thing she wanted was a man disrupting her well-ordered life. After the accident, it had taken her years to reestablish some sense of control over her own fate. She would not relinquish that control easily.

He was, however, only asking her to use his first name. And, really, what could be the harm? Calling him Todd was hardly tantamount to falling into his arms. She'd already done that and though she still blushed when she thought about it the world in general hadn't come to a screeching halt. Only her own had tilted on its axis. No members of the Board of Education had called for her resignation. As long as she continued in the future to resist the sexy, come-hither glances that made her knees go weak, she saw no reason not to give in on this one little point.

Besides, she decided practically, it might help to relax him. Although he'd looked entirely too pleased with himself for being precisely on time when he'd picked her up at eight o'clock, since then he'd grown increasingly tense and withdrawn. He'd taken out half a dozen cigarettes over the last twenty miles, toyed with them, then ground them out. He'd lit none of them.

Now he looked more like a man driving to his own execution than a father going to get a little help for his son. Maybe if he knew more about what to expect, he'd ease his grip on the steering wheel and his foot off the accelerator. The wispy Australian pines along the edge of the road were zipping past at a dizzying pace.

"Okay, Todd," she said, finally. He turned a wicked, thoroughly satisfied smile on her. Her pulse took off faster than a jet trying to make up time. "Would you like me to tell you a little about what to expect at Dolphin Reach?"

The smile vanished at once, replaced by cool indifference. "Whatever," he said, his voice flat, his gaze instantly focused straight ahead.

She tried not to feel disappointed at the lack of enthusiasm. "I think you're going to like Ann," she began conversationally. "She has a brilliant mind and she's wonderful with people. She's especially good with kids. She should have had half a dozen of her own. Not that she hasn't made up for it. She's foster mother to a whole passel of kids with special needs.

You know, the ones who are hard to place for adoption. A couple of them have had problems with the law. I'd be a little afraid to take on a kid like that, but not Ann. They seem to respond to all that love. Not a one has been in trouble again.''

Her lengthy recitation was met by brooding silence. Still determined to overcome his anxiety, she rattled on, describing Ann's special kids, her educational background, the house she'd built along a little spit of land that jutted off one of the Keys below Islamorada.

''It started out as just an ordinary little two-bedroom, one-bath beach house, but then she started finding these kids. The third bedroom was tacked on when she took in Kelly and Michael. The fourth bedroom and the second bath came the following year. I think she's up to six bedrooms and three baths now and if there were more land, she'd probably add two or three more. She's a real pushover for a kid with a problem.''

''Sounds like a generous lady.''

The complimentary words had an odd, sarcastic edge to them that made her want to spring to Ann's defense. ''She is,'' she said curtly instead and fell silent.

Todd would just have to see for himself. She knew he was uptight about this meeting, but she hoped he wasn't planning on being rude and difficult with Ann. Then she smiled. Ann would snap the arrogant starch right out of him, if he tried it. Her smile grew wider. She could hardly wait.

Suddenly he jerked the wheel and turned into a McDonalds. "Coffee," he said when she glanced at him. From his defensive tone, she had a feeling he expected an argument.

"Sounds good," she said cheerfully, recalling Ann's prediction. The woman was an absolute, mind-reading wizard. Thank goodness, she was fully prepared to counter any argument Todd might mount to avoid finishing the journey to Dolphin Reach. She armed herself for battle.

When Todd blinked at her easy acceptance of the delay, she had to turn away to keep him from catching her confident grin. When she looked back, though, the defiant glint in his eyes hadn't quite vanished. He was pulling into a parking space, rather than the drive-through lane. "Let's go inside."

She bit back a reminder that they had another hour's drive ahead of them. "Fine."

The sun was burning away the last of the fog as they walked across the parking lot. The temperature was already climbing. Liz was glad she'd decided on shorts and a T-shirt, despite the early morning chill. Already it was too warm for the sweater she'd tossed over her shoulders at the last minute.

Inside the restaurant, Todd ordered coffee and a full breakfast for himself, then glanced at her.

"Just coffee."

When they were seated, he bit into his egg sandwich, grimaced and pushed it away. He slouched down in the booth, dominating it, his long legs sprawling. Liz had a hard time keeping her gaze off the bare, muscular length of them. Why had she told him to dress informally for this meeting? She should have known that Todd in shorts and a polo shirt would send her pulse into overdrive. She watched the play of muscles in his thick arms as he stirred his coffee, then took another bite of the sandwich. He looked as though he were being tortured. She could identify with the feeling.

She dragged her gaze away from those strong, blunt fingers that she knew from experience were capable of incredible gentleness. She took a sip of coffee.

"How's your breakfast?" she asked innocently.

"Fine."

"Yes. I can see that."

Apparently detecting the amusement in her voice, he regarded her warily.

"Why did you order it?"

"I was hungry."

"Really?"

He finally shrugged sheepishly. "I guess I wasn't as hungry as I thought."

"Or were you just stalling?"

"I thought the woman we're going to see was the psychologist," he growled.

"She is." She grinned at him. "She'll also tell you that I frequently practice without a license. As long as I don't charge, they probably won't lock me away for it. Even so, I prefer to think of it as offering unsolicited advice. It's less risky. Now that we've analyzed my bad habits, what about yours? Why are you stalling?"

"I'm not crazy about psychologists," he admitted, the way some people confessed to a dislike of tarantulas and rats. His adamant tone startled her.

"Have you had much experience with them?"

"Enough."

The curt response was a dismissal, if ever she'd heard one. "Maybe you'll tell me about it some time."

"Don't count on it."

The remark was said with such cold finality, Liz felt as though he'd slapped her. Over the last couple of days, she'd tried very hard to keep herself from thinking of Todd Lewis as anything more than a parent of a troubled student, but the memory of his touch had lingered. Her imagination had taken the tenderness of his comfort, the fire of his caress and soared on a less restrained journey. The man might not have much respect for her opinions, but he had desired her in a way that had stirred old, forgotten longings. For a few minutes in her classroom, she'd been reminded of what it felt like to be stirred by a woman's passions, to feel the sharp tug of yearning for a man's embrace.

Now, with those four abrupt, chilly words—*don't count on it*—he'd relegated her to an annoyance, someone he had to placate but not trust. Well, he could just take his moody, overbearing attitude and stuff it, she thought furiously. She glared at him.

He caught her expression and sighed. He ran his fingers through his hair. "Look, I'm sorry. I'm on edge. You know how I feel about all of this. If it weren't for Kevin and what you said about his failing, I wouldn't be here.''

She tried to understand his misgivings, but it was as if there were some vital piece of information missing. She settled for simply acknowledging them. ''I know that. Maybe you should stop thinking of this as some sort of an ordeal and consider it a chance to widen your horizons, try new things.''

He chuckled. ''Throwing my words back in my face, aren't you?''

''The occasion seemed to call for it.''

''Okay, let's go. I'll behave. I will even try not to treat this friend of yours like she's some sort of dragon.''

Liz smiled knowingly. ''Oh, but Ann is a dragon, the genuine fire-breathing variety, especially when it comes to kids in trouble. Don't get any ideas about conning her with your charm.''

''I never even considered it.''

Her eyebrows rose skeptically. ''In a pig's eye.''

''Hi, Liz!'' The shouted greeting came from somewhere behind a pile of yellow rain slickers. A blond—no more than twenty or twenty-one, Todd guessed—poked her pixie face above the pile and waved. ''Annie called. She's running late, as usual. Tommy or one of the kids took exception to having oatmeal for breakfast and threw it across the kitchen. She's overseeing the cleanup.''

''Has Alexis given birth yet?'' Liz called back.

"Nope. Poor thing. She's down at the end. Go on out and scratch her belly. There's a bucket of fish on the dock. You can give her a few if she behaves."

"How will I know if she's behaving?"

"You'll still be dry."

As they wandered toward the docks behind Dolphin Reach, Todd studied her with a bemused expression. "Are we actually going to visit a pregnant dolphin?"

She grinned at him, her eyes sparkling with sheer delight. He couldn't recall ever having seen quite that look on her face before. He wished he and not some temperamental dolphin had been the one to put it there.

"Why not?" she teased, racing on ahead. The subtle sway of her hips was enough to make him forget what he'd asked. Who cared about a dolphin—pregnant or not—when a woman clad in a pair of sexy white shorts and a surprisingly provocative T-shirt was within view. He'd be willing to bet she'd thought the walking shorts sedate, the loose T-shirt unrevealing. They weren't, he thought with a wild skittering of his pulse as she leapt down onto the dock.

"Hurry," she was urging, just as Todd was wondering if he shouldn't dive straight into the icy waters and cool off. His libido was becoming as overactive as Hank's.

Dazed, he simply followed her, only partially aware of the dolphins who swam close, then stood on tail fins as if to bob a friendly greeting. When he caught up with Liz, she was kneeling on the end of the dock crooning to a huge dolphin. The seeming absurdity of her actions was lost on him. All he could think about was the way her attractive little butt was poking into the air. That rear would just about fit into the palms of his hands.

"Come meet Alexis," she said, as if introducing people and dolphins were an everyday occurrence. "Alexis likes company. Ann says she's been upset because she can't do as much with the kids these days. She's impatient for the baby to be born so she can get back to serious playing."

He knelt down beside her on the dock. "There's a contradiction in there, but I don't dare try to challenge it." He smiled at her. "I see that you and Alexis are old friends."

The dolphin seemed to beam in agreement, then slid into the water and swam away. A moment later, she leapt into the air with an odd sort of lumbering majesty, before diving back with hardly a splash. Back at the dock, she waited for Liz's applause and her reward.

"That was wonderful, Alexis, but don't you go getting overly excited," Liz chided as she dropped a handful of fish to the eager dolphin's mouth. She leaned down and rubbed the slick snout, then turned to Todd with a delighted grin. "Isn't she beautiful?"

"As dolphins go, I would have to say she is particularly impressive," he said dryly.

Liz turned back to the attentive Alexis. "Did you hear that, Alexis? He thinks you're impressive. That's quite a compliment from a man of his no doubt discerning taste when it comes to women."

"Sweetheart, when it comes to women, I prefer them a little sleeker than Alexis here, preferably with two legs. And," he added as an afterthought, "I definitely do not want them pregnant."

"Sssh. You'll hurt her feelings."

"Do you always get like this around the dolphins?" he inquired curiously.

"Like what?"

"Let's just say you seem to have lost all your inhibitions."

She gave him a pert smile. "Not all of them."

"Too bad."

"Don't let her kid you," a voice said from behind them. "Underneath that stern, classroom manner of hers lies the heart of a pushover."

Liz blushed to the roots of her red hair. Interesting, Todd thought, as he stood up to meet the woman who'd just joined them. Tall and raw-boned, she had short, dark hair and bright blue eyes that sparkled with intelligence. Her features were irregular but interesting. It was the warmth and humor in her expression that made her beautiful. She radiated an inner joy that was both contagious and reassuring.

"You must be Todd," she said, taking his outstretched hand in a firm, no-nonsense grip. "I'm Ann Davies. I'm so glad you and Liz were able to drive down this morning."

"So am I," he said and found, amazingly enough, that he meant it.

"Sorry I'm late, but the kids..." She shrugged. "I'm sure you know how that goes."

"Of course. We haven't been here long."

"No. We stopped for breakfast in Key Largo," Liz said and the two women exchanged a conspiratorial look.

"Am I missing something here?"

"Not really," Liz said. "Ann had warned me that she'd lost a lot of prospective clients in Key Largo."

He grinned. "I see. No wonder you were able to read my mind. You'd been coached."

"By an expert," Liz agreed. "Why don't the two of you go get acquainted and talk about Kevin? I'll stay here with Alexis."

Suddenly an old familiar feeling of dread engulfed Todd. "Aren't you coming with us?"

Ann shook her head and linked her arm through his. "I think it'll be better if you and I talk first. Liz can join us later."

Without waiting for him to agree, she turned on her heel and strode off toward the main building. Inside, she waved him to a comfortable sofa, then gestured with a pot of coffee. When he nodded, she poured two cups, then handed him one of them.

"So, Todd. You don't mind if I call you Todd, do you?"

He chuckled. "No. I only wish Liz would do it as easily."

"She has a very strong sense of what's right and wrong in professional conduct."

"I've noticed."

She glanced at him sharply. "You object?"

"Not the way you mean. It's just…inconvenient at times."

Ann's quick bark of laughter echoed off the walls. "I'm sure you find that part of the challenge."

He felt his face flame. "Maybe I do."

She looked him over assessingly. "I wish you luck," she said quietly, but with apparently heartfelt sincerity. Todd felt as if he'd passed an important test without really understanding why it mattered.

"Now, then," she went on briskly, "tell me about Kevin."

His defenses slammed back into place. Filled with reluctance, he began to describe his son. Ann listened and absorbed without comment. It was a seductive technique. Before he knew what was happening and very much to his surprise, he found himself talking about Sarah, as well.

"Kevin was only four when she left. For a long time I was terrified I'd never be able to make it up to him."

"Why did you feel the need to try? Had you caused her to walk out?"

"No. Not directly, though I'm sure there were things I could have done to make things better. But what Sarah really wanted was freedom and excitement. She hadn't expected the ordinariness of marriage. She didn't want to be tied down to running a house and taking care of a kid. Sometimes I'd get home at night and find her practically hysterical."

"Did she tell you why?"

"She said she couldn't cope—not with the marriage, not with Kevin."

"So he was a problem, even then?"

"I didn't think so," he said defensively.

"But Sarah did."

"Yes."

She paused long enough to make a few notes on the legal pad in her lap, then met his eyes with a direct, unflinching gaze. Todd realized then that in just the short time they'd been together he had come to trust her.

"I want to meet Kevin," she said. "Can you bring him down, say, the same time next weekend?"

"You're going to test him?"

"There are a few standard tests I can do to see how he processes information. Mainly I want to talk to him, find out what's been happening with him in school as he sees it. Often that tells me as much or more than the tests do."

"And then?"

She smiled at him. "Why don't we just take this one step at a time? Let's see what I learn next week and make a decision then."

Todd nodded.

She stood then and went to her desk. When she joined him again, she had several forms in her hand and Todd felt his insides twist.

"If you'll just fill these out," she said, handing them to him along with a pen.

He bent his head over the papers and read them slowly and carefully. He painstakingly went over the fine print. Finally, when he was finished, he nervously filled in the requested information and signed them with his usual bold and virtually illegible scrawl.

As he handed them back to Ann, he caught the speculative look in her clear blue eyes. "Why didn't you tell me?" she said softly.

Todd stiffened at once. "Tell you what?"

"Why didn't you mention that you're dyslexic, as well?"

Chapter Six

Shocked, Todd simply stared at Ann Davies.

"Why would you say that?"

She smiled compassionately. "I am right, aren't I? You do have dyslexia?"

Feeling utterly defeated, Todd sighed and sank back on the sofa. "How did you know?" he asked.

"I saw how you struggled with the form. Added to your defensiveness about Kevin's situation, it made sense. Did you have treatment when you were a child?"

He shook his head. "Not really. Oh, there was endless testing, but once my parents realized I wasn't the perfect son they'd anticipated they pretty much gave up on me. I struggled along and did the best I could."

"But you hated school," she guessed.

"I couldn't wait to get out. I stuck it out through high school, even though I was twenty when I graduated."

"If it was so terrible, why did you stay?"

"Because I figured I'd have to have that damned, meaningless diploma to get anywhere."

"Graduating from high school is hardly meaningless, especially under the circumstances. It was a tremendous accomplishment. You should have felt very proud."

"It is hardly an accomplishment if you still can't read worth a damn and only earned the diploma by outlasting the system."

"Liz doesn't know, though, does she?"

He shook his head. "No, and I don't want her to."

"Why on earth not? It's nothing to be ashamed of. No one knows exactly what causes dyslexia, but it is not indicative of either intelligence or character."

"No, it's not," he agreed. It was the one thing he'd worked like hell to prove, especially to himself. "I've carved out a niche in the world, proved to all those educational hotshots that I'm not the stupid kid they thought I was. That doesn't mean it's not a terrible drawback. I sure don't want it to become common knowledge that I can't even read half the contracts I sign."

"Telling Liz is hardly the same as having it become common knowledge. She'd understand."

"And I would feel like less than a man."

Ann waved that aside with a derisive snort. "That's probably the dumbest thing I've heard you say all afternoon."

His chin set stubbornly. "If you tell Liz, our deal's off."

She shook her head, her smile a little sad. "I don't think so. You'd never deprive your son of the opportunity to get a good education just because of your own ridiculous macho pride."

"Are you willing to test me?"

"No," she said easily, "but not because you're threatening me, Todd Lewis. I'll keep it between the two of us, because I think you're the one who ought to tell her. I hope you'll do it soon. Liz has had to deal with enough secrets in her lifetime."

Ann's words lingered long after he and Liz were back on the road. He wondered what she'd meant by the secrets that had affected Liz's past. Keeping his own counsel about his dyslexia seemed like such a little thing. It only mattered to him. Surely his reticence on this one thing wasn't something that would ultimately come between them.

If Liz noticed how distracted he was, she kept silent, apparently attributing it to a natural reaction to the meeting with the psychologist. He blessed her for her intuitive understanding and kept his eyes trained on the road, until he spotted the place they'd decided to stop to pick up lobsters to take home for dinner.

He wheeled into the sloped gravel driveway and slammed on the brakes. For the first time since it was the macho thing to do in high school, he felt like getting rip-roaring drunk so that he could forget all about secrets and the past.

When Todd pulled into the jammed parking lot beside the ramshackle fish house, his jaw was still set at a mulish angle. Liz had been biting her tongue all the way up the road to keep from asking him what had gone on in his meeting with Ann. It was enough that the two of them seemed to have gotten along. Even more important, Todd had agreed to come back with Kevin the following week. With their business taken care of, they were free to... to do what? The possibilities made her as skittish as a teen on her first date.

Warning herself not to start thinking like an adolescent ninny, she followed Todd across the parking lot, her steps slowing as they neared the building. Though the screened-in porch sagged and the handwritten menus were grease-stained, Liz knew the appearance of the weathered wood structure was deceptive. On weekends the place was crowded with Miamians and tourists looking for an inexpensive, informal place to sit by the ocean, sip a few beers, listen to a little music and eat some of the best seafood in the Keys. Though it was only four in the afternoon, the heavy throb of a live band filled the air. It was a sultry, provocative atmosphere.

"Let's get a beer before we pick up the lobsters," Todd suggested as he held her door open for her.

"We really should be getting back to Miami," Liz protested, giving in to her jittery nerves. "You know how this road is on Saturday nights. We'll be caught in bumper-to-bumper traffic if we wait much longer."

He shrugged off her concern with a wave toward the narrow highway. "The traffic is already bumper-to-bumper. How much worse can it get? Come, on. Just one beer. Besides, I like the group that's playing this afternoon."

"We could probably still hear them halfway home," she muttered, giving up. It was clear they wouldn't head north until Todd was ready to go. She was surprised he'd even bothered to ask her wishes, when he had no intention of complying with them.

"Smile," he leaned down and whispered in her ear. "This will only hurt for a little while."

She scowled at his back as he led the way through the restaurant to the porch in back. He found a table in a corner far away from the band, signaled a passing waitress for two beers, then sat down across from her.

"Great, isn't it?"

"Terrific." She caught the sarcasm in her tone and flinched. To be perfectly truthful, it was lovely. Sunlight set off diamond sparklers on the ocean's smooth surface. A soft, languid breeze barely stirred the air, which was fragrant with the tang of salt and the coconut scent of suntan lotion. The noise was a happy blend of laughter and music, albeit a little loud for her taste. Guiltily, she glanced across at Todd and caught the frown on his brow as he watched her.

"Sorry," she said, knowing how absurd it was to be this nervous in the presence of a man who'd proved his kindness. He was hardly likely to seduce her in the middle of the restaurant, even if half the couples on the dance floor did seem to be engaged in some sensually explicit movements that barely qualified as dancing. Just watching them made her blood heat up and her glance skitter nervously away from Todd's. Ridiculous, she told herself sternly. How often did she get to the Keys? Not nearly often enough. She might as well enjoy it, now that she was already here.

"I didn't mean to snap," she apologized. "I like it here." Even as she said the words, she felt herself begin to relax. She smiled. "Really."

Todd nodded in apparent satisfaction. As she watched, his tension seemed to ease slightly. "Good. You need to relax more. Today with the dolphins was the first time I think I've ever seen you completely at ease."

The memory of the very pregnant Alexis lumbering into the air in a bid for attention brought back another smile. "How can you watch those dolphins and not relax? I know it's just a quirk of nature that they appear to be laughing, but it's contagious. I wish we'd brought Kevin along. He would have loved them."

"I'm glad we didn't," Todd said so softly she could barely hear him over the swell of music.

"Todd . . ."

"Don't say it," he said with an odd sense of urgency that sent shivers along her spine. "I don't want to talk about Kevin or his education right now. For the next couple of hours, this is just between the two of us."

Liz felt her heart slide straight down to her toes. "It can't be," she managed to say in a choked voice.

"Yes," Todd said stubbornly. "Just the two of us."

Before she could argue with him, he jumped to his feet and held out his hand. "Come on. Dance with me. They're playing our song."

"Our song?" she repeated, feeling dazed and all too intrigued. The beat was demanding, unrelenting and sensual, just like Todd. "I don't even recognize that song."

"Neither do I. If we dance to it, though, we'll make it ours. We'll never be able to hear it again without thinking of this moment and this place."

The softly spoken words were those of a romantic, but the look in his eyes was pure rogue. Despite herself, Liz responded to the pull of the words and the look. Her heart accepted the sweet tenderness of the thought. Her body throbbed to the promise of the look. She stood up and followed him to the tiny square of floor where several other couples were already gyrating to the pulsing beat.

Todd danced with a surprising lack of self-consciousness, his hips and shoulders creating a suggestive taunt that Liz unconsciously matched. As they circled and dipped, his gaze clashed with hers, holding her, teasing her. The brush of his hip against hers as he whirled her under his arm set off an explosion of desire. Whether it was that alone or merely the quick pace of the music, Liz couldn't be sure, but she was breathless and filled with an odd sense of expectation. She was almost disappointed when the music ended and Todd released her hand.

The lull in music lasted no more than an instant. Todd flashed a silent question at her and Liz found herself nodding. He laughed and the last of the shadows in his eyes fled. "I knew you'd lose yourself to this, once I got you out here."

"Don't be so smug," she retorted, but she felt too much happiness welling up inside to stay irritated for long. It had been far too long since she'd let herself go like this. The last time she'd been on a dance floor, she'd agreed to chaperon a junior-high party with a friend who taught at the school. One of the ninth graders had asked her to dance. He'd barely reached her chin and he'd moved with more dogged determination than grace. It had been nothing like this. Todd turned fast dancing into a subtle mating ritual. Heaven knows what he'd do with a slow song. It would probably be for the best if she never found out.

Fortunately, she supposed, this particular crowd was only interested in music that soared, in beats that never slowed. Her hair was a damp, uncontrollable mess and her cheeks were flushed by the time Todd finally led her back to their table. She drank her now-warm beer in a single gulp.

"Another one, please. Very cold."

Todd's eyebrows shot up at the request, but he waved the order to a waitress and the beers were on the table in icy plastic mugs within minutes. She was just catching her breath.

Then she looked into Todd's eyes and felt the earth open up. No man had looked at her like that in years. She hadn't wanted one to. She still didn't. The heady thrill was too confusing, too dangerous. That intimate, possessive look shook her hard-won serenity the way King Kong had rattled Manhattan skyscrapers. It was an unthinking gesture on his part, probably something he indulged in all the time. A man as sexy as Todd Lewis did not sit around on Saturday nights watching his hibiscus blossom. Flirtations were probably as commonplace for him as they were foreign to her. All of which meant that she ought to stop drinking this beer at once, stay off of the dance floor and if at all possible pretend that he had the sex appeal of a turnip.

She pushed away the icy beer, regarded the dancing couples wistfully and sighed. She figured at best she had a shot at two out of three. A glance across the table assured her that Todd was no turnip and no amount of vivid imagery on her part was going to turn him into one.

"Maybe you'd better get the lobsters now," she said reluctantly.

He seemed startled by the sudden request. "Is something wrong?" He reached across the table and ran his finger across her frowning lips. The sandpapery warmth of his work-roughened touch sent tingles skyrocketing through her. "You're frowning."

Good, she thought crazily. It was very good that he couldn't tell that her well-educated brain was turning to mush and her karate-trained knees were quivering like so much raspberry Jell-O. A little more internal heat from his touches and she'd melt into a happy little puddle right at his feet.

"The lobsters," she reminded him breathily.

He still seemed puzzled, but he nodded. "I'll go get them."

While he was gone, Liz drew in enough deep breaths to restore oxygen to her apparently deprived brain. Oddly enough, she didn't seem to be thinking any more clearly by the time Todd returned with the cooler of lobsters.

"One more dance," he said, putting the cooler down on the floor and holding out his hand.

Liz nodded and got to her feet before realizing that the music had gentled to a slow, intimate caress. It whispered seductively and her pulse throbbed in awareness as Todd's arms went around her. His strength inflamed her femininity. The heat of his body enveloped her in longing. His purely masculine scent, a combination of salt and musk with a lingering hint of soap, made her thoughts careen wildly to images of provocatively tangled limbs and dampened skin. She wanted to run from those images. She wanted to indulge them.

She wanted to live them.

It was the last, the desire to tempt fate, that urged her closer into his embrace. Resting her cheek against his damp shoulder, she sighed with the sheer pleasure of being held. The thunder of Todd's heartbeat matched the cadence of her own, swift and dangerous. She ignored the warning, indulging in the wild temptation, oblivious to consequences beyond this moment. She felt young and beautiful and cherished in these powerful arms. She felt even more when she looked into the hazel depths of his eyes, heard his harsh intake of breath. Desire, as demanding and insistent as anything she'd ever experienced, overwhelmed her, took her breath away.

She clung to Todd and let herself simply feel for once. She might regret the moment later, but not now. His hand, already low on her back, swept lower. Their hips fit together in an instinctive joining that shocked her with its intimacy. When she would have pulled back, Todd's whispered protest stopped her.

"Don't start thinking. Just enjoy the moment," he pleaded. "Let me hold you."

She sighed and relaxed against him. They were barely swaying to the music now, barely keeping up the pretense of dancing. She heard the warning voices begin again in her head, a whisper at first, then louder. It was only when she felt the tug on her arm that she realized the warnings weren't entirely in her imagination.

"Watch it," a couple said, pointing down as shouts and laughter erupted around them.

Dazed and bereft without Todd's arms to hold her, Liz glanced down. Lobsters—she had no doubt at all they were the ones Todd had just bought—were skittering crazily across the wooden planks in every direction.

She choked back a laugh at the startled indignation on Todd's face as he tried to round up the creatures who were making a madcap, if somewhat direction-less, dash for the sea and freedom.

"Let them go," she said as laughter bubbled up. He looked at her as if she were crazy.

"Do you know how much I paid for those things?"

"Let them go. They've made a daring escape. They deserve to survive."

"But dinner?"

"I'll fix pasta. It's just as well. I'd never have been able to throw them into a pot of boiling water, any-way." She shivered. "Do you realize how cruel that is?"

"I never thought about it. I suspect if we thought too hard about killing cows or pigs or chickens, we'd never eat those again, either."

"It's not the image I mind so much, it's the action. Beef and chicken get to the stores in neat little pack-ages wrapped in cellophane. They are not mooing and clucking in my presence. Those lobsters were going to be staring at me with their beady little eyes when I plunked them in the pot. The pasta will be much bet-ter."

"Okay, Miss Humanitarian," he said with amused tolerance, "do you want me to carry them back to sea or shall I leave them to their own devices?"

Since one of them was heading directly for the bare toes of a woman seated near the bandstand, Liz said, "I think you'd better help them along. No telling where they'll end up, otherwise."

Several of the other customers joined in the lobster chase and the whole crowd descended to the beach for an impromptu ceremony setting them free. When the last of the lobsters was out of sight, Todd turned back to her. The look in his eyes made her breath catch in her throat. He stepped closer and slid his arms around her waist.

"You're going to owe me for this," he said in a whisper that sent chills down her spine.

She lifted her face and discovered that his lips were barely a hair's breadth away.

"What?" she murmured.

"This will do nicely," he said, his mouth covering hers.

Startled, Liz's hands hung limply at her sides as those velvet lips brushed hers with fire. Her toes curled into the cool sand and her body swayed toward Todd's. As he had for those few moments on the dance floor, he became the center of her universe, the pull of gravity that drew her at will. The kiss was sweet and gentle. Though she was sure he meant it to be unthreatening, it shook her to her very core.

Romantic seductions on the beach weren't her style, especially not with the parent of one of her students. Sanity struggled against yearning and slowly but inevitably won. Determined not to let him see how deeply he had affected her, she stepped out of the embrace and faced him with a jaunty smile. That smile would earn her an Academy Award in Hollywood. It was the best acting she'd ever done.

"Next time we have a school fair, I'll know what price to put on my kisses," she said, linking her arm casually through his.

The breezy comment drew a scowl. "What the hell's that supposed to mean?"

"I'll put a sign on the booth: One kiss—three lobsters or equivalent in cash."

He regarded her disbelievingly. "You actually sell kisses at a damned school fair?"

"It's better than being dunked."

He shook his head. "I can see I've been missing a lot by skipping those fairs."

"We raise a lot of money," she said proudly.

"I'll just bet you do." He stalked off to the parking lot, leaving her to scurry along behind.

She hadn't guessed, until he spun out of the parking lot, just how mad he was. They were all the way to Key Largo by the time he spoke again. "No more."

"No more what?"

"No more selling kisses to a bunch of old fools who should be home with their wives."

Liz laughed. "They're usually with their wives. It's all in good fun, for a good cause. Some of the money is for school projects and the rest goes to the homeless."

"I'll match whatever you made in your best year, but I will not have you sitting in a booth getting paid for granting kisses."

Liz's sense of humor began to fail her. She felt her temper begin to rise. "You don't have anything to say about it."

"Like hell," he muttered and lapsed once more into silence.

When they got to Liz's house, he sat stonily behind the wheel.

"Are you coming in for pasta?"

"I don't think so."

"You realize, of course, that this entire argument is ridiculous."

"Probably."

"Then why are we having it?"

A sheepish expression stole over his hard features. "Because I'm a pigheaded, possessive jerk."

"Agreed."

"You didn't have to agree so readily."

He looked so hurt that she found herself laughing again. "Okay. I can't say I found anything in your self-analysis with which I strongly disagreed, but I will promise not to rub it in if you'll come in for the dinner I promised you."

He still seemed reluctant.

"We can finish making plans for Kevin," she said.

Todd shook his head. "If I come in, I guarantee you that Kevin is the last thing we will discuss."

Liz swallowed hard. There was no doubt in her mind exactly what he was thinking. And wanting.

"Then maybe you'd better go," she whispered.

He put a finger under her chin and turned her to face him. "Do you really want me to?"

Dozens of conflicting emotions whirled through her, colliding like bumper cars. She blocked them all out finally and went with her heart.

"No."

He swallowed convulsively. "Are you sure?"

She gave him a tremulous smile. "Don't push your luck, Todd."

He sighed at that. Gentle fingers brushed a curl off her cheek, then lingered along the curve of her neck.

"I'd better go."

Dismayed, she stared at him. "Why?"

"You're not ready, sweetheart. I'm not ready for a one-night stand and you're not ready for anything else."

The truth of that slammed into her gut and brought her out of the sensual reverie that had led to her impulsive invitation in the first place. She leaned across and brushed a kiss on his forehead. "Thanks," she said, hurriedly opening the door as if she couldn't escape fast enough now that she'd been reminded of the stakes of the game she'd been playing.

"I'll call you tomorrow," he promised.

"Don't."

"We have to talk about Kevin, remember."

She sighed. Kevin, again. He was their link. The only one. All during the long, restless night, she tried to remember that. Instead, all she felt was the burning wake of desire left by Todd's kisses.

Chapter Seven

The horrible sound of metal grinding against metal rent the air. Tires skidded and screeched on wet pavement. Glass shattered. Screams. Sirens. More screams, hers, lodged in her throat. Not her baby! No, please God, not her baby!

Heart hammering, her body soaked with perspiration, Liz awoke with a start to the sounds of thunder, rain and a frantic pounding on her front door. Before she could reconcile nightmare and reality, the doorbell rang, followed by more impatient pounding. She sat up in bed, jerked the covers around her and blinked, trying to drag herself awake and away from the pull of the familiar, haunting dream.

Even though she couldn't quite get herself moving to respond to it, that incessant pounding had been a blessing. It had ended the nightmare before she had actually seen Laura lying in the street. For weeks after the accident, overcome with guilt and grief, she had relived the horror night and day. Finally, she had been able to block it consciously during her waking hours, but not at night. Still not at night.

Her whole body shaking from the inside, she drew in a ragged breath and tried to get her act together to answer the door. She was normally a morning person, up by six, fully alert by the time she left for school at seven. The routine never varied. Even on weekends she was usually quick to waken at disgustingly early hours. Today she felt as though her brain were made of oatmeal.

She reminded herself that she also usually had more than one hour of sleep. Last night, with Todd's touches etched indelibly on her skin and in her imagination, had been the pits. It had been nearly dawn by the time she'd fallen into a restless sort of half-slumber. It was barely after seven now. It would take a powerful amount of adrenaline to convert oatmeal into functioning brain cells after that amount of sleep.

"Liz, are you in there? Dammit, open this door before I break it down."

Todd? She shook her head and tried to imagine why Todd would be beating on her door at the crack of dawn on Sunday. The doorbell chimed several more times. She'd never before realized quite how loud it was.

"Elizabeth Gentry, open this door!"

The heavy oak door rattled on its hinges. Liz flew out of bed, grabbed an oversized Miami Dolphins jersey and pulled it over her head as she ran through the house.

"I'm coming, for heaven's sake." She rolled her eyes as she caught sight of her disheveled appearance in the full-length mirrors on the dining-room wall. It was too late to do anything about that. She threw open the door. "Todd, what on earth are you doing? Trying to wake the dead?"

He simply stared at her, breathing heavily, his brown hair soaking wet. "In a manner of speaking," he said softly, his gaze covering the distance from tousled hair to bare toes in less time than it took to check out fruit for bruises. It was a quick examination for reassurance, not a leisurely survey of masculine interest.

Even half asleep, she recognized the genuine panic in his haggard face, the relief that filled his eyes. "What's wrong? Are you okay? Has something happened to Kevin?"

"No, no, we're fine. It's you."

"Me?" She might be more befuddled than usual but he was making no sense, at all. Maybe his brain was waterlogged. It was really pouring out there and the sky was pewter gray with not a glimmer of blue in sight. It was a perfect day for huddling under the covers and sleeping in. Not likely, she thought with regret.

"What's wrong with me?" she said, still trying to make sense of Todd's unexpected arrival.

"Liz, I have been calling here ever since I dropped you off last night. I thought we ought to talk about what happened. First the phone was busy, then there was no answer. I called all night long."

Liz thought of her own sleepless night and decided there was something perverse in a universe that kept two people wide awake and apart, when they could have been doing much more interesting things together. She simply shook her head and waved Todd inside. She headed for the kitchen and left him trailing along behind, dripping all over the tile floor and muttering under his breath. When she'd put the coffee on, she leaned against the counter and regarded him curiously.

No one had ever worried about her before. Not even Ed, during the three years of their college courtship or the five years of their marriage. He'd thought her capable and confident and had left her to her own devices more often than not. He'd never even opened a door for her after their first date. If Ed had called and no one had answered, he would have shrugged it off. He might have mentioned it later. He might not. There were reasons for his blasé attitude, but she hadn't known that until later. Much later. Still, it meant she didn't quite know how to handle Todd's unexpected and entirely unwarranted protectiveness.

"Liz, you still haven't answered me."

"I'm not sure I should."

"What?"

"If I explain this time, then you'll think you had the right to ask. Not that I'm not flattered you were worried, but I've been living my own life for a good many years now. I'm not used to having my activities questioned."

"Activities?" he repeated blankly. Then, "*Activities!*"

She laughed as a crack of thunder seemed to emphasize his indignant expression. "Cool your jets, Mr. Lewis. Not those kinds of activities, though that wouldn't be any of your concern, either."

"I'd better sit down," he said, pulling out a chair at the kitchen table. He rubbed his eyes, then ran his hand across the dark stubble that shadowed his face. He was even sexier with the unshaven look. It was odd how that worked, Liz decided. Some men simply looked like bums with a day's growth of beard. Todd was definitely not one of them.

"Do you have any idea how worried I was?" he was saying with a touch of asperity.

She dragged herself back from thoughts of sexy faces, in general, and Todd's, in particular. "I'm sorry. As you can see, you had no reason to be."

"Then why the hell didn't you answer the phone?"

He looked so bewildered that she decided to relent. "It was unplugged, at least the one in the bedroom was. I often do that, if I want an uninterrupted night's sleep."

"You get a lot of calls in the middle of the night?"

"Occasionally the kids like to play pranks, usually when one of them is having a slumber party. They think it's fun to call the teacher in the middle of the night. Last night was apparently one of those nights.

The phone was ringing when I walked in. After two more calls asking whether my refrigerator was running, I decided to pull the plug.''

"Your refrigerator? Some kid wanted to know about your refrigerator?''

She chuckled. "Surely, you know that one. They ask if it's running. When you say yes, they tell you to go out and catch it. It's as old as the hills. There are more. Want to hear them?''

"Spare me.''

She patted him on the shoulder sympathetically as she poured him a cup of coffee. "Maybe after you've had some caffeine.''

"And eggs?'' he said, casting a hopeful look at her. "I never did get around to dinner. Or would you rather go out for breakfast?''

"I'd rather get some sleep,'' she said. "But I guess that's out of the question.''

The slow, lazy grin he directed at her was pure seduction. His eyes fell to her bare legs that were only minimally covered by the loose-fitting football jersey. "Well...''

"Never mind,'' she said dryly, an unmistakable and infuriating catch in her voice. "I'll fix eggs. Where's Kevin?''

"He spent the night with a friend.'' A look of horror spread across his face. "You don't suppose...''

Liz chuckled. "More than likely he's the culprit, or at least a willing coconspirator.''

"I'll wring the kid's neck.''

"It's a phase. He'll grow out of it.''

"If I decide to let him live that long. It's inconsiderate."

Liz pulled eggs from the refrigerator, along with milk, butter and bacon. "How do you want the eggs?"

"Done."

"Thank you. That's very helpful. For that you will get one egg scrambled and only one strip of bacon."

"I want at least three of each. I'm famished."

"Too much fat and cholesterol."

"Thanks for worrying."

"Don't mention it."

"I'll settle for two eggs, but I still want three strips of bacon."

She shrugged. "They're your arteries." She slapped the bacon into the microwave, put the bread in the toaster, then cracked the eggs into a bowl and whipped them with an easy efficiency she thought she'd all but forgotten. Big breakfasts had seemed all too lonely since... She slammed the brakes on the thought.

When the steaming food was on the table, most of it in front of Todd, she took a deep breath and said, "You want to tell me why you decided it was so important that we talk last night? You're the one who walked away from my invitation to stay."

Todd choked on a bite of egg. Odd, she thought, especially since he was the one who'd brought it up and made it seem so all-fired important. Maybe he didn't like being reminded of foolish decisions.

"Now?" he said.

"It's as good a time as any."

"Okay." He pushed his plate away and tipped his chair back on two legs. "I wanted to try to understand what's happening between us."

"And you thought that was something we could figure out on the phone in the middle of the night?"

"We sure as hell can't seem to do it when we're together. Every time I'm in the same room with you, all I want to do is make love to you."

Liz choked at that. Todd patted her on the back—none too gently—and grinned. "You asked."

She cleared her throat. "So I did."

"Anyway, I thought we might be able to talk more sensibly on the phone. Then when I couldn't reach you, I thought you might have been even more upset than I'd realized by what's been happening. I know it goes counter to your professional ethics. I know I've probably been pushing too hard. Last night you admitted that you wanted me, too, and my guess is that that threw you. Then I turned around and rejected your offer. It's all pretty confusing."

"That's putting it mildly." She regarded him curiously. "Why are you pursuing this, Todd? Because I'm not available? Is it the challenge?"

"I quit worrying about making difficult conquests years ago. I leave that to Hank now. He thrives on the chase."

"But there must be hundreds of women in Dade County who would kill for the chance to go out with you."

"None like you," he said with what sounded like total sincerity.

"Please," she retorted disbelievingly.

"Liz, you're beautiful, compassionate, intelligent. Surely I'm not the first man to be attracted to you since your husband died."

She shrugged off the compliment, unwilling to let him see that it pleased her. "I've been asked out."

"Have you gone?"

"A few times."

"Why not more?"

"No one's interested me. I'd rather spend the evening with a good book than a lousy date."

"But I do?"

"I haven't accepted a date with you yet, either," she reminded him with a teasing grin.

"Technically. But we do have a way of winding up in each other's arms. A lot of the best planned dates don't end up that way. I'll ask you again, why me?"

She looked up from her breakfast and met his gaze evenly. The daring glance cost her. She felt instantly mushy and vulnerable. She didn't like the sensation one bit. That didn't keep her from admitting honestly, "I don't know."

His smile was rueful. "And I gather you're not happy about it, either."

"Sorry."

"So, what are we going to do about it? Last night you were willing to sleep with me. Did that also mean that despite your misgivings you're ready to see if what we're feeling is real?"

"Real?" The very word made her nail-biting nervous.

"You know, the happily ever after variety of attachment."

"There's no such thing," she said succinctly and with feeling.

"I'll admit I've had serious doubts myself, but how do you account for all those golden anniversaries that Willard Scott mentions on the 'Today' show?"

"Probably sheer inertia."

She caught the momentary shock in Todd's eyes. His tone more cautious, he said, "And what we're feeling is ...?"

"Lust," she said without hesitation. "It doesn't take a genius to figure it out. We don't have to spend weeks analyzing it to death. It happens to the best-intentioned people. Just remember that lust is like an itch. You scratch it, it goes away."

"And if it doesn't? Does that mean it's love?"

She shook her head and said softly, "I think love is a myth."

Todd's chair hit the floor with a resounding crash. "Okay, Liz, where did all that cynicism come from?"

"Experience," she said bitterly.

"But your marriage?"

"I don't want to talk about my marriage." She stood up and began slamming dishes into the dishwasher. She did it with such force she was surprised some of them didn't break. The fact that she'd opened up this particular can of worms annoyed the dickens out of her. Why hadn't she turned Kevin's problem over to a school psychologist or a social worker, anyone? Why had she insisted on getting involved? Because she'd had no idea that Todd Lewis would get under her skin so, that's why. Now it was too late.

"I'm sorry you were hurt and I'm sorry if talking about it is still painful, but I don't think we have any choice," Todd persisted, ending any hope she had of being able to curtail the subject.

"Why?"

"So we can get beyond it. Weren't you in love with your husband?"

She frowned, turned on the garbage disposal and let it grind for an unnecessarily long time. When she clicked it off, Todd was still waiting. "You might as well answer," he said softly.

"Okay, dammit. Yes, I was in love with my husband."

"He didn't love you?"

She was flattered by his shocked tone. Suddenly resigned, she found herself letting the words pour out.

"Oh, I thought Ed loved me," she said. "Maybe he did at first, while we were still in college and in love with all the possibilities of life. He respected me. He treated me well. Laura and I never wanted for anything that really mattered. There were no huge fights. In fact, there was very little passion, at all."

Stacking the pans and utensils in the sink, she tried very hard to keep her tone indifferent, her manner cool.

"I can't believe that," Todd protested. "You're one hell of a sexy lady."

Once more, the compliment seemed to give her the courage to go on. "At the time I would have argued with you," she confessed. "I thought I was probably frigid, that I didn't make sex interesting enough. It wasn't until the day he died that I realized that the reason our relationship was so lukewarm was because Ed had been seeing another woman for almost the entire time we'd been married. Even his family knew it, but none of them told me. When I accused them of covering up for him, they didn't deny it."

He muttered a curse under his breath. "How did you find out?"

"Laura, our daughter. You know how three-year-olds are. They say the first thing that comes into their heads, even when they've been sworn to secrecy."

Todd's shock registered in the widening of his eyes. Honest eyes, eyes that could never conceal secrets. "Your three-year-old child knew her father was having an affair?"

"She hardly knew the details, but she had met *Aunt* Caryn. She told me all about her. She had no idea that the woman wasn't a real aunt or that in telling about her she was tearing out Mommy's guts. Poor naive Mommy."

Todd moved to stand beside her, his expression sympathetic. She couldn't bear that look. Pity was the last thing she wanted from Todd. She just wanted him to understand why she would never again trust a man, why she didn't believe in love, why there would never be anything serious or permanent between them.

"When I confronted Ed, he admitted everything. He said she meant nothing to him, that she was simply good in bed, that I was the woman he wanted to be married to, the woman he wanted as the mother of his children. I guess I was supposed to feel flattered that he trusted me in this important role, sort of a glorified brood mare and hostess for the rising young doctor.''

"You said you found all this out on the day he died. What happened?''

"Laura told me all about her Aunt Caryn when she and Ed came home from what was supposed to have been a trip to the grocery store. They'd made a detour by her apartment. Apparently it was her birthday. He'd taken her a diamond necklace.''

She picked up the skillet in which she'd cooked the eggs and scrubbed it with a vengeance. The scouring cleaned the pan, but did nothing to wash away the memories of her incredulity when she'd discovered the full extent of his treachery.

"Can you imagine? We were still struggling to pay for Ed's medical education and his office setup. It was a big deal for me to get a cubic zirconia pendant on our budget and he bought her a diamond necklace.'' She slammed the pan in the drainer.

"So you confronted him.''

"You bet your life I did.''

Even now she recalled her fury as she'd cornered Ed in the family room and questioned him until he'd admitted everything about the relationship.

"Had it been a fling I might have been able to forgive him, but after five years it could hardly be called that. I told him to get out, that I wouldn't play second best to a whore, that I wouldn't have a woman like that around my daughter. Do you know he was actually offended that I would call her that? He defended her. Then he went and packed a suitcase. I sat in here with a glass of Scotch, which I hate by the way, and tried to get myself under control." Her hands stilled in the soapy water. Her voice shook. "It wasn't until he was out the door that I realized he had Laura with him."

If possible, Todd looked even more horrified by that than by anything that had been revealed before. "He was taking your daughter?"

She nodded and felt the tears beginning to well up. "I tried to go after him, but by the time I grabbed my car keys, he had a pretty good head start. He was always an irresponsible driver and apparently the knowledge that I was coming after him made him even more reckless than usual. I was about a mile from here when I heard the crash." She buried her face in her still wet hands as the sounds echoed in her memory for the second time that morning. Tears mingled with dishwater.

"You have no idea what it was like. I knew it was Ed, even before I got to the accident scene. In my heart I knew it. It was as if I'd died."

Leaning against the counter, she felt Todd's arms go around her. She leaned back against the solid comfort of his chest. Her tears flowed unchecked.

"They were both dead when you got there?" he asked.

"Laura was. He hadn't taken the time to make sure she was fastened into her car seat. She'd been thrown

from the car. She was just lying there... Oh, God,"
she whispered, as the remembered horror engulfed her.
"My baby was just lying there."

When Todd turned her around in his arms, she
fought to regain control. "I'm sorry. I don't know
what's gotten into me. I haven't cried so much over
this since it happened." She had just relived it, again
and again, ridden with guilt, convinced that if she'd
left it all alone, if she'd ignored Ed's adultery the way
so many other wives did, her baby would still be alive.

"Maybe you should have cried long ago."

She shook her head. "It wouldn't have changed
anything. At least you can see now why teaching is so
important to me. It's all I have left. It's what I'm
suited for. Each year those kids become my family. I
won't do anything to put it at risk."

"And you think a relationship with me would do
that? Or is it just that you're afraid to risk another relationship? I know all about fear, Liz. I know what it's
like to be betrayed and angry and determined never to
let it happen again. I went through it when my wife
left."

Her spinning emotions seemed to still as Todd's
words sank in. "Your wife left you?"

"She didn't want to be with me. She couldn't cope
with Kevin. I'm just beginning to understand that her
complaints about Kevin's behavior might have had
some basis in fact, but I still can't forget what she did.
She abandoned a four-year-old boy."

"How horrible. I can't imagine a woman doing that. I'd give anything, anything, to have my baby back again."

"The point is we can't change the past, Liz. I'm just beginning to see that we have to go forward, to take risks or we might as well give up on life. I've protected myself ever since Sarah left, steered clear of emotional involvements, but I can't seem to do it with you. Maybe that's the way love works. It slips up on you when you're finally ready and then there's nothing you can do to fight it."

"This is not love," she said determinedly. The word terrified her. "It can't be."

He caressed her cheek. The expression in his eyes was gentle and understanding, but equally determined. "Call it whatever you like. All I know is that you're already in my heart. Now that I've found you, I'm not going to let you go. I didn't want to have these feelings, but I do. I won't ignore them."

"If we sleep together, it will end."

"No," he said, touching his lips gently to hers. "It will just be the beginning. Wait and see. I'm not Ed. I'm not going to turn to someone else."

Todd made the promises with confidence, but he worried. Not about his own feelings, but Liz's. She'd admitted she wanted him, that the attraction was mutual. But her faith in men was obviously shaky, and for good reason. What would happen when she found out that he wasn't the man she thought he was, when she learned that he was less than perfect, that things she took for granted in her life were next to impossible for him?

He had seen the shelves of books in the family room, the leather-bound editions that looked like classics, the brightly jacketed current fiction. What would she think if she knew that he couldn't read them, could barely struggle through the morning headlines? What would they do when she realized that something so important to her was something they could never share? And worse, that he'd kept the truth of it from her?

He wasn't sure if it was her fears or his doubts that, in the end, kept him from pushing for a commitment. Liz's affection for Kevin was strong, and she knew all of his problems. But that didn't mean she wanted to take them on on a permanent basis in both the child and the lover. He had been right to keep his dyslexia a secret. No matter what Ann thought about her friend's ability to understand, he didn't trust Liz's feelings enough to risk it. She could run, just as Sarah had.

Time was the answer...if she would give it to them. He was afraid to ask for himself. He asked for Kevin.

"Will you go to the Keys with Kevin and me next weekend?" he said.

She saw right through the ploy and shook her head at once. "You've met Ann now. You two will be fine in her hands. You don't need me."

"We do. I do." He grinned. "Remember, I still have to get past Key Largo."

Before he could wrangle an agreement from her, the phone rang. With a pitifully grateful expression, she grabbed for it. Her relief quickly turned to surprise. "Yes, he's here. Just a minute."

She held out the phone. "For you."

He heard the mild censure in her voice, guessed her intentions as she turned away and caught her before she could leave the room. He held her wrist tightly until he felt her relax, then slid his hand down to encompass hers. He rubbed his thumb in circles on her palm as he listened to Hank.

"Sorry to track you down, partner, but we've got a problem."

Todd was instantly alert. "What?"

"All this rain has turned the site into a sea of mud. I got worried and stopped by. It looks to me like we might be in trouble. The garage foundation could be slipping. I think you'd better get over here and take a look. We sure as hell don't need to have this garage tumbling down and injuring somebody."

"I'll be there in fifteen minutes. Thanks, Hank."

"You have to go," Liz said unnecessarily. There was no doubting the relief he read in her eyes.

"For a while. That was Hank. He thinks we could have a problem with the garage construction. He's already there."

"How did he know where to find you?"

"I left the number on the message on my answering machine, in case Kevin called and needed me."

The set of her lips indicated she still wasn't exactly pleased, but she merely nodded.

"Have dinner with us later," he suggested.

She withdrew without moving an inch. The shuttered expression in her eyes was unmistakable, even before she said, "No, Todd. I'm exhausted. I don't want to go through all this again."

"We won't. Not tonight, anyway. I'll ask Hank to join us. I'd like you to get to know him. We've known each other since we were kids. We've worked together since the beginning. I'm sure he has a date he'll bring along. Kevin will be there. You'll be properly chaperoned. No serious talk, just a pleasant evening at my house. Steaks on the grill, that sort of thing."

"More cholesterol," she chided.

"If I make it chicken, will you come?"

"It's Sunday night. I usually grade papers," she protested, but he could tell she was weakening.

"You have all afternoon to do the papers. We won't make dinner until seven."

"You aren't going to give up, are you?"

"No."

"Okay, I'll be there."

"Terrific."

He jotted the address on a piece of paper, then pressed a quick, hard kiss across her lips before taking off. He wanted to get away before she could change her mind.

Or before he thought about exactly how little she had on under that damned Dolphins jersey.

Chapter Eight

"So, old buddy, I thought you weren't interested in the sexy teacher," Hank said the minute Todd joined him at the shopping-center site. Though his expression was cautiously neutral, his voice was thick with innuendo. It took every ounce of Todd's restraint to keep from punching him. Only exhaustion and the fact that Hank outweighed him held him in check. After all these years, he should have grown used to Hank's baiting. Today, though, because it involved Liz, it annoyed him more than usual.

"Tell me what makes you think the foundation for the garage might be slipping," Todd said tightly.

"Don't want to talk about her, hmmm? Interesting."

"Hank, don't you have anything better to do than to speculate on my love life? I assure you it's incredibly boring compared to yours."

"Hey, I'm just curious. It's been a long time since I've discovered you at a lady's house at the crack of dawn on a Sunday morning. I thought you were the one who was worried about her reputation. Not that I plan to squeal on the two of you, of course. That's not my style. My mama taught me never to kiss and tell."

"I think the more appropriate lesson here would have to do with tattling," Todd said wryly. "Just for your information, though, I did not spend the night at Liz Gentry's place, if that's what you're implying with your usual lack of good taste. I went by this morning."

"To share a couple of sweet rolls and the Sunday paper, no doubt." The innocent words were delivered with a healthy amount of masculine skepticism. Todd clenched his fists.

"Contrary to your limited range of thinking, Riley, not every male-female relationship is based on sex," he said. Goodness knows he wished this one were, but Hank would have to subject him to torture before he'd ever admit it.

"It is possible," he told his inherently lecherous friend, "for two people of opposite sexes to be friends."

Hank poured himself a cup of coffee and regarded Todd doubtfully. "And that's what you and Kevin's teacher are? Friends?"

"Exactly." It was only a tiny white lie, aimed at protecting the lady's honor. He'd had those same kiss-and-tell lectures Hank had.

"It wasn't so many days ago the two of you were standing right here shouting at each other. Some of my best dates don't arouse that much passion. If that's what you call a friendly discussion, maybe I need to develop a new technique."

"We had a slight disagreement. Things change. If you don't believe me, you can see for yourself. I was planning to ask you to join us for dinner tonight at my place."

"Whoa," Hank said, a knowing grin spreading across his face. Todd considered once more rearranging that face. "First breakfast. Now dinner. I'm impressed. Now you'll never convince me this isn't serious."

"Hank, the only thing serious around here this morning is the likelihood that I'm going to hold you face-down in the mud until you scream for mercy," Todd snapped. He realized he was grinding his teeth. "Now do you want to come for dinner or not?"

"I wouldn't miss it, buddy. Anything I can bring?"

"A date, and a zipper for that smart mouth of yours. If you insult Liz, I'll start proceedings in the morning to dissolve our partnership. The only engineering job you'll be able to get will be in the far reaches of some very distant country that nobody can even pronounce, much less locate on a map."

The threat fell on deaf ears. Hank draped an arm around his shoulders and poked him playfully in the

chest. His eyes sparked with mischief, just as they had
during their hell-raising adolescence. Despite his current discomfort at being the object of it, he usually
enjoyed Hank's irreverent humor.

"You are so-o-o cute when you're angry," he
taunted Todd. "No wonder the teacher lady is crazy
about you."

With a muttered oath and a glare, Todd stomped
out of the trailer and splashed through the mud to the
garage. He had a sinking feeling that tonight was
headed for disaster.

Liz spent the whole day wondering how she had let
Todd manipulate her into this dinner. For a woman
with very definite ideas about what she did and did not
want in her life, she seemed to be losing sight of that
clear vision. She didn't want to go. She didn't have
time to go.

She could hardly wait to get there.

Even though he hadn't asked her to bring anything, she had made a key lime pie. Crumbling the
graham crackers for the crust and squeezing the key
limes kept her hands occupied, if not her mind. Her
thoughts reeled like so many leaves caught up in an
autumn breeze.

These meetings between them, except when they had
to do with Kevin's progress, had to stop, she decided
as she poured the filling into the pie shell. They were
too volatile. They had her doing and saying things she
immediately regretted, things that were totally out of
character.

Just this morning, for instance, she had known she ought to go and change out of that provocative football jersey. She'd never thought of it as sexy, only comfortable. Then she had seen the way Todd's gaze lingered at the sweep of faded material over her bare breasts. She had felt her stomach turn inside out as he'd glanced with increasing frequency at the bare expanse of her legs below the too-short hem. And, dear God in heaven, she'd enjoyed it. Too much, in fact. She'd deliberately refused to change because Todd's masculine appreciation had made her feel sexy in a way that Ed's technically expert lovemaking never had. Lust did astonishing and dangerous things to common sense, she thought, running her finger around the inside of the bowl and licking the filling off her fingers in an unconsciously sensual gesture.

Tonight, though, she would tell him flatly that the flirtatious games, enjoyable though they were, were over. She didn't have to explain. It was enough to say that that was the way she wanted it. Todd was a gentleman. He wouldn't force the issue. And even if he tried, there was very little he could do without her cooperation. He was too busy to invent ways to spend time with her, if she wanted to be elusive.

Despite her resolve, she found herself dressing in a becoming turquoise sundress that was rich with colorful embroidery at the off-the-shoulder neckline. Her sandals were the merest scraps of turquoise leather. It took her twenty minutes to get her makeup exactly right. She balked when she found herself reaching for an outrageously expensive bottle of per-

fume on her dresser. Ridiculous. She'd just vowed that
Todd would never get really close to her again, cer-
tainly not close enough to appreciate seventy-five-
dollars-an-ounce perfume. She shrugged finally and
dabbed the scent on her wrists and behind her ears. At
least if she planned to say goodbye, she might as well
make sure he'd remember her.

Todd's house wasn't at all what Liz had expected.
It was old and like Ann's it wandered with haphazard
charm. The nooks and crannies inside would be a
child's hide-and-seek delight. Built of Dade County
pine, it was situated on a Coconut Grove lot that was
overgrown with palm trees, hibiscus and towering
banyan trees. From the narrow, winding, well-shaded
street it was almost impossible to tell that the house
even existed.

Once inside, though, she discovered that it had been
made comfortably modern without losing any of its
original character. The colors were bold and practical. The clutter was exactly what you'd expect from a
single parent and an eight-year-old boy. There were
toys scattered over the floor of the den, papers lit-
tered the top of the huge desk, a magazine had been
discarded in a chair; and a pair of sneakers was lying
in front of the sofa with one sock nearby. Idly, she
wondered about the location of the other sock.

It was the back patio area, though, that took her
breath away. Complete with a pool that blended into
the landscape, it was a lush tropical paradise. It was a
setting meant for seduction and Liz shivered as she

imagined swimming there, alone with Todd, on a starlit night.

When she reached the terrace, Hank was already there. There was an impertinent gleam in his blue eyes when Todd introduced them. His appreciative gaze swept over her and he sighed dramatically.

"Too bad old Todd here saw you first," he said regretfully as he took the pie and gave it an approving once-over before placing it on the redwood table that was set for five. "You're just my type."

"As long as they're over the age of consent, they're your type," Todd countered. "Watch him, Liz. He's an inveterate flirt."

She laughed. "And you're not?"

She wasn't sure which of the males was more startled by her assessment. As Todd started to launch an injured protest, she caught a spark of curiosity in Hank's expression, a closer examination. In that instant, she realized that whatever else these men might be—business partners, healthy competitors with the ladies, opponents on a tennis court—they were friends. Surrounded mostly by women at school, she hadn't spent a lot of time observing the traditional rituals of male bonding, the backslapping buddies who played cards or sports or simply hung out sipping beer and discussing life, but she recognized deeply ingrained loyalty when she saw it. With a single look, Hank had displayed a protectiveness toward Todd that she admired, even as it left her shaken.

A petite blonde in silky purple designer pants and a scanty yellow bandeau top emerged from the house just then and Hank's attention slid away from Liz. The woman draped herself around Hank. His thick, powerful arm circled her bare waist in a friendly hug as he made the introductions.

"Gina here is an investment banker," he said.

Liz took another look at the woman she'd been about to dismiss as a cute bit of expensively clad fluff and caught the shrewdness in her eyes. Gina was grinning at her as if she knew exactly what Liz had been thinking. She wanted to die of embarrassment, as she gave herself a stern lecture on the dangers of stereotyping.

"Have you two been dating long?" she asked, envying the fact that they seemed so comfortable together. Perversely, after all her good intentions of the afternoon, she suddenly wanted Todd's arm around her shoulders. She felt a sharp pang of longing for the feeling of belonging it would impart, but he'd gone inside for the rest of the food.

"Ages," Hank said in response to her question about his relationship with Gina.

"You realize that to Hank anything longer than two hours is ages," Todd commented from the doorway as he returned with a platter of chicken ready for the grill.

"Not so," Hank protested, his expression wounded. "I've known Gina for three weeks, ever since I asked her to go over my portfolio."

"And it took you twenty days to get her to go out with you," Todd reminded him, winking at Gina.

"She's obviously more discerning than most of your dates."

"Cruel, partner. Are you trying to ruin this for me?"

Gina laughed, seemingly unaffected by the harmless bantering about Hank's flirtations. She patted his bearded cheek consolingly. "Don't let him get to you, honeycakes."

"Honeycakes?" Todd and Liz repeated in unison. Liz couldn't imagine anyone even daring to call the burly giant of a man by such an endearment. Hank looked chagrined.

"I will never live it down," he muttered, grabbing the chicken. "Let me tackle a manly task before my image is destroyed."

Gina turned to Liz. "Do you have any idea why it's considered manly to cook over a grill, when you probably couldn't get him to do the exact same thing at a stove? I know for a fact that he has never, ever cooked anything more complicated than a boiled egg."

"Perhaps it's simply a genetic defect," Liz suggested.

"No doubt."

The whole evening went like that, filled with fast quips and easy laughter. Kevin put in a brief appearance, long enough to eat, then went back to his room to play video games. He seemed to take Liz's presence in stride. He withstood Hank's friendly teasing, responding in a way that gave Liz an entirely new perspective on Todd's friend and business partner. For all of his pretended indifference to commitment, Hank fit neatly into Todd's small family. Surrogate uncle, pal, whatever, he belonged. Again, Liz felt a subtle yearning tug at her.

When the rain came back, the air cooled and they all retreated indoors. Todd pulled Liz down beside him on the sofa and rested his hand lightly on her bare shoulder in a gesture that was both comfortably right and exciting. The light caress of his fingers played havoc with her good intentions.

It would be easy to get used to this, she thought as the conversation swirled around her. The warmth, the open friendliness, Todd's casual intimacy were all too alluring. It would be dangerous to believe in this, to believe it could last.

If Todd was to be believed about Hank's tendency to roam, Gina was all too likely to be replaced by next weekend. Was her own relationship with Todd any less tenuous? Not likely. No, this was definitely not something to count on for more than the moment.

It was Hank who broke up the party, mentioning an early day and the problems at the site that he and Todd had identified that morning and now needed to rectify. Liz suspected that the polite excuses had very little to do with his desire to go. She'd seen the exchange of heated glances between him and Gina. They might be leaving at a respectable hour, but she doubted that their evening would end. To her amazement, she found that she was jealous.

She glanced at Todd as he was saying goodbye, wishing that for just one night she could abandon her common sense. She'd almost done it last night, but

Todd had stopped her. Would he do it again? It would be foolish to even consider finding out. By the time he came back into the living room, she had begun straightening up.

"You don't need to do this," he told her. "Sit with me awhile."

"Really, I don't mind. If you don't do it tonight, you'll be kicking yourself in the morning. With two of us, it'll take no time at all to get things in the dishwasher. Then I have to go."

"Liz."

His fingers caught her chin. As he forced her to face him, her lips parted involuntarily. Todd's face was only inches away. "I've wanted to do this all night," he said, just before his mouth closed over hers.

Her pulse leaped erratically as wishes came true with wicked accuracy. The kiss was all she'd longed for, tender and intimate, hungry and demanding. She gave herself up to it, savoring, clinging and demanding in turn. Whatever else he might be—domineering, manipulative rogue came immediately to mind—he was also one heck of a kisser. She felt as though the floor were dropping away below her feet, then realized that he'd scooped her into his arms and was carrying her. Where? Did it even matter?

Of course it did, she thought, snapping back to reality. Her eyes opened wide as he sank down onto the sofa, settling her into his lap.

"I haven't necked in a very long time," he said, as if he found the prospect both intriguing and amusing.

Liz had to admit to a certain longing to recall the sensations herself. "We can't do this," she protested weakly.

"Give me one good reason," he said.

"Kevin."

"I checked. He's asleep."

"He could wake up."

"He's a sound sleeper," he said, sprinkling quick little kisses up the side of her neck. He nipped her earlobe, then ran his tongue inside. She shivered all the way down to her toes. A kiss like that was worth a little risk. She turned her head for the full effect. How was this man able to slide past her defenses? Why did her judgment seem to fail at his slightest caress?

Todd's hand slid around her waist, then up, slowly, deliciously until it cupped her breast. The peak was already throbbing. His touch set off an aching sort of pleasure that rippled down to settle in her abdomen. Her back arched and she longed for Todd's hand to follow the downward path of those devastating ripples. Her whole body was tense with the wanting of that touch and the fear that it would lead to more than she could handle.

Thankfully—she supposed—it was not to be. Slowly, his caresses stilled. The kisses went from leisurely and passionate to quick and innocent. Her flesh burned just the same, but she was coming back to earth, back to a reality that included test papers to be graded and a long drive home.

"I have to go," she said, more shaken than she cared to admit.

"I wish you didn't. I'll follow you to be sure you get home safely."

The gentlemanly offer touched her. "You can't do that. I don't want you to leave Kevin alone in the house. I'll be fine."

He studied her intently. "Will you really?"

"Absolutely."

"I'm talking about more than the drive home, Liz."

"I know. I'll be fine on all counts."

"And you'll go with us on Saturday?"

Her smile was wobbly. Mrs. Elizabeth Gentry would never smile that way, would never even consider continuing this relationship. She had made that decision quite rationally just this afternoon. As for Todd's Miss Liz? She obviously had a reckless streak that matched the unexpected daring in his soul.

"You mount an incredibly effective campaign," she admitted, weakening.

"Irresistible?"

"Irresistible," she confirmed reluctantly.

"I'll pick you up at eight again."

She nodded.

"I'll call during the week."

She nodded again.

"Dream about me tonight," he said as he tucked her into her car.

Liz refused to answer, but she could tell from the devilishly certain look in his eyes that he knew she would.

Chapter Nine

I'm not going!" Kevin's voice rose in a wail.

Todd stared at him, startled by the vehement outburst. Just last night Kevin had been excited by the prospect of spending a day in the Keys. For the past week he'd taken the idea of meeting Ann Davies in stride, or so it had seemed. Maybe he'd just needed desperately to feel optimistic about Kevin's attitude.

"You are going," Todd said firmly, as he grabbed a striped polo shirt out of the batch in the dryer and looked it over. Thank goodness, it wasn't too horribly mussed, even though it had been left in overnight. Todd hated washing and ironing, which was why they always seemed to get done at the last possible minute when every piece of clothing and towel in the house was dirty.

"Put this on," he said, holding out the shirt.

"No." Kevin crossed his arms over his bare chest.

"Kevin!"

"No," he said again, taking off for his room. Todd heard the door slam behind him. His heart sank.

Carrying the shirt, Todd walked slowly through the house, trying to decide how to handle this tantrum. He was already fighting his own demons about the day's plans. He wasn't prepared to do battle with Kevin, as well. After a brief struggle to control his temper, he tried the door. Kevin had locked it from the inside.

"Son, I want you to open this door," he said in a low, barely controlled voice. When there was no sound from inside, his voice climbed a notch. "Now!"

"I won't do it. I won't go," Kevin whimpered tearfully. "You can't make me."

"We both know I can. Now open the door and let's talk about it."

Finally the key rattled in the lock. Todd turned the knob and stepped inside. He held out the shirt. "Put this on."

Kevin's eyes shimmered with tears and his lower lip trembled. He shook his head. Todd sighed.

"Son, put the shirt on," he said wearily. "Then we'll talk about this."

When Kevin remained right where he was, Todd tugged the shirt over his head and struggled to get his arms through the sleeves. Kevin offered limp resistance. "You know, son, when we talked about this last night, I thought you understood why we were going to the Keys today."

"I don't want to go see some dumb old psychologist," he said, his expression mutinous.

"Then tell me why you feel that way."

"No. I just won't go."

The stubborn refusal cost Todd the last of his patience. He grabbed Kevin around the waist, hefted him into the air and carried him across the room.

"Sit," Todd said, plopping him down on the unmade bed. He sat down beside him. "We've been talking about this all week. This is not some sort of punishment. Dr. Davies is going to try to help you, so you won't have so much trouble with your schoolwork."

"I'm doing better," he mumbled. "Mrs. Gentry said so."

"That's true, but you could improve even more once we know exactly what the problem is. Isn't that what you want?"

"I guess."

"Then what's the problem?"

Kevin kept his eyes downcast. Todd saw tears begin to run down his cheeks. His heart constricted. It took every ounce of his self-control to keep from going into the other room and calling Liz to say that the trip was off.

"Son, talk to me. You know you can tell me anything. Are you afraid?"

Kevin shook his head.

"Then what?" Todd asked, feeling increasingly helpless.

"Dad, aren't you proud of me anymore?" Kevin said in a tearful, scared voice that broke Todd's heart.

"Oh, Kevin," he said, his voice catching.

He should have realized how it would seem. He should have known that after a lifetime of unquestioning support even when grades slid, Kevin would see this as a sign of betrayal. He pulled him into his arms and tried to quiet his heartbroken sobs. For a fleeting moment, as he hugged Kevin close, he resented Liz for driving a wedge between him and his son; for getting them involved in this wasted exercise.

Then he thought of how different his own life might have been if someone had really worked with him. Oh, he'd accomplished a lot, more than he'd had any reason to expect, but there might not have been nearly as many scars. No matter what his reservations might be, they had to give this a try.

"Dad!" The protest was long-suffering. When Kevin wriggled to get loose, Todd gave him one last hug, then ruffled his hair.

"Sorry. I just want you to know that that is something you never need to worry about. I am very proud of you," Todd said, letting him go with a little pang of regret. Sometimes he missed the days when Kevin had been willing to cuddle in his lap and watch TV until he fell asleep. Those days had given him such a feeling of completeness, as if he'd spent his whole life just waiting to be a father. He'd vowed to do it all so differently from the way his own father had.

"I will always love you and be proud of you," he said earnestly, praying that his words were getting through. "As long as you're doing your best, I can't ask for anything more. Dr. Davies may be able to help you do that."

"But why can't Mrs. Gentry? I like her. She's made the other kids stop laughing at me. I haven't had a single fight, Dad. Not even one."

"And I'm sure she appreciates that, son. She knows how hard you're trying. But this learning disability stuff is not her specialty. She is going with us today, though. Dr. Davies is her friend. I met her last week. She's every bit as nice as Mrs. Gentry."

"Who cares if she's nice?" Kevin grumbled with another spark of resentment. "It's Saturday. Why do I have to take a bunch of dumb old tests on Saturday? If she really cared about me, she wouldn't make me do that. I wanted to play baseball."

"You can play baseball tomorrow."

As the realization that his father was not going to relent finally sank in, Kevin sighed in resignation. "Will I have to go next Saturday, too?"

"I don't know. If she wants to work with you, we'll have to work out the arrangements."

"Try to make it so I don't go on Saturday. Okay, Dad? Please."

"I'll do the best I can," Todd said, grateful that this first battle appeared to be behind them.

He could still recall exactly what it had been like for him being dragged from psychologist to psychologist, usually after school and on Saturdays. If his reading deficiency hadn't made him feel different enough, his inability to participate in other activities had only served to emphasize that difference. While other boys played Little League games, he sat in sterile waiting rooms and looked at papers he couldn't understand. It seemed as though every time he finally got to join a team, his parents heard about some other doctor, some new program.

He had actually been relieved when his parents had given up on him. At least, he'd been able to get involved in sports again. He'd become a first-class swimmer, winning meets around the state. The successes had been the only bright spots in an otherwise dreary adolescence.

Kevin was every bit as good as he had been. They swam laps together in the backyard pool most evenings. Kevin was like a little fish, already competing in local swimming meets and picking up ribbons. Todd had a feeling if things worked out and Kevin got a chance to swim with the dolphins, he wouldn't be able to keep him home from the Keys. So far, though, he hadn't told him about that aspect of the program for fear Ann wouldn't take him on as a client.

It was exactly eight, when he pulled into Liz's driveway, Kevin sitting stoically in the backseat. Before he could even cross the lawn, Liz was coming out the door carrying a picnic basket. The sight of her cheerful expression chased away the last lingering traces of resentment. She might have forced his hand in this, but she'd only had Kevin's interests at heart. He knew that with absolute certainty.

"What's this?" he asked, taking the heavy basket from her.

"Breakfast. Fresh-squeezed orange juice, a Thermos of coffee, warm Danish and milk for Kevin."

He chuckled. "Taking no chances that we'll get sidetracked in Key Largo, huh?"

She looked up at him innocently. "I just thought this would be so much healthier than anything we could get along the way."

"Right."

As they headed down U.S. 1, Todd was increasingly grateful for Liz's presence. While he toyed nervously with unlit cigarettes, she kept Kevin occupied with an imaginative variety of games designed for car travel. There was nothing condescending about it, either. She played along with him with enthusiasm. By the time they'd passed through Tavernier, even Todd found himself relaxing and joining in.

They were almost to Dolphin Reach, when Kevin propped his chin on the back of the front seat and asked hesitantly, "What's going to happen when we get there, Dad?"

"You mean with the tests?"

"Yeah. Will they be hard?"

Todd remembered only the frustration, the repeated sensation of failing. He couldn't recall anything about the actual content. Nor was he willing to admit in front of Liz that he even knew what to expect. Besides, he thought defensively, the tests had probably changed dramatically over the last twenty years or so. Ann hadn't shown them to him and he hadn't asked.

"Kevin, this is nothing for you to worry about," Liz intervened. "It's not like school, where you get a grade. Dr. Davies only wants to see why you're not doing well. That'll tell her how to go about helping you. Lots of students your age come to her with exactly the same kind of problem."

"You mean they can't read, either?"

Todd heard the amazement in Kevin's voice. Perhaps he needed to hear that he wasn't alone. God knows, it might have made a difference with him. He'd thought for years that he was the only one struggling to make sense of his assignments. Once more Liz had said exactly the right thing. If only she hadn't hinted that Ann Davies would accept Kevin into her program. There were no guarantees of that. Nor was there any evidence yet that what she offered would be the best treatment for Kevin's difficulty.

He himself had been to dozens of experts and no one had ever set out a plan for helping him. Everyone had agreed that there was a problem, but they'd all seemed more fascinated by identifying the cause than by finding a solution. The methods for correcting it had been as varied as the number of psychologists he'd seen.

First his parents were told to help him with his schoolwork. Then, they were told to make him do it on his own, even if he failed. Another one thought he should be removed from regular classes. Yet another insisted he should remain in the mainstream and be held back, if necessary. He fell two grades behind and grew angrier with each passing year.

As Liz cheerfully expounded on the excitement at Dolphin Reach, Todd's irritation with her lack of sensitivity mounted. If she kept on, Kevin would be horribly disappointed if Ann turned him down.

"Liz, let's just get through the testing," he snapped. His short-tempered comment had both Liz and Kevin staring at him. "Sorry. I just don't want Kevin counting too heavily on this."

Until he saw Kevin's face fall, it hadn't occurred to him that he'd just suggested the possibility of another failure. Silently, he cursed himself as Kevin sat back, subdued for the rest of the trip. Liz looked as though she wanted to take Todd's head off, but she bit her lower lip and kept quiet. When they arrived at Dolphin Reach, she was the first one out of the car.

Ann met them as they crossed the parking lot. She looked tired and disheveled, but she was smiling warmly. Liz hugged her and introduced her to Kevin. After hanging back for a minute, Kevin responded just as Todd had to Ann's quiet questioning and interested attention. By the time they had walked into the building, she had Kevin chattering away. At the door to her office, she dismissed Todd and Liz.

"Go see Alexis," she ordered. "She's had the calf. If she were any prouder, she'd be handing out cigars."

"But," Todd protested, looking pointedly at Kevin.

"Kevin and I will be just fine," Ann responded. "Go."

With a last reluctant glance, Todd followed Liz outside and down to the dock. He was spoiling for a fight, but she didn't even give him a chance to throw the first verbal punch. As she had the previous week, she bounded on ahead. She was kneeling down for a closer inspection of the newest dolphin by the time he arrived.

"Isn't this the most beautiful dolphin you've ever seen," she enthused, her eyes flashing with excitement. Her earlier irritation with him seemed to be forgotten.

Like babies, Todd thought the tiny dolphin looked pretty much like all the others. He knew better than to say it. "Exceptional," he confirmed, biting back his desire to snap at her, to snap at anyone.

Liz apparently caught the tautness in his voice. She glanced up at him pointedly. "Do you want to explain what's wrong or do you plan to take my head off the rest of the morning? If you can't think of something pleasant to say, maybe you should just go back inside and wait in the lobby."

He closed his eyes and sighed. When he opened them again, he dropped down beside her on the end of the dock. "I'm sorry. It just worries me to see Kevin getting his hopes up. This program of Ann's may or may not be right for him. Even if she does take him on, it's going to be a slow process. Kids tend to expect overnight miracles."

She rocked back on her heels and put her hand on his thigh. It was meant as no more than an impulsive gesture of apology, but Todd felt the blood begin to pound through his veins.

"Okay, maybe I was overselling it a bit," she admitted. "I'll try to be more careful. Just don't let your doubts rub off on Kevin. He needs to have a little hope."

He lifted her hand to his lips and kissed it. "Deal," he said, his gaze locking with hers.

Liz seemed troubled as she withdrew her hand. She started to speak, then fell silent. Before he could press for an explanation, Alexis apparently tired of being ignored. She began chattering for attention. Liz leaned over to rub her snout, then reached out to stroke the calf that was right at Alexis's side.

Todd watched the interaction with something that felt strangely like envy. She was so affectionate with Kevin, even with the dolphins, but around him there was still so much reserve. How could she melt in his arms one day and be so distant the next? Still, the idea of being jealous of a dolphin was clearly absurd. Observing them, he found himself grinning.

"Careful, Liz. Alexis seems to be a little nervous. Are you sure you should be hovering quite so close to the calf?"

"Don't be silly," she said, stretching a little further to pet the baby dolphin. "She knows I'd never..."

The words died in a sputter as Alexis tumbled Liz straight off the dock and into the icy water. She bobbed up, hair streaming and indignation written all over her face. Todd pulled out the camera he'd tucked in his pocket and began taking pictures.

"Don't you dare," she said, scrambling back onto the dock.

He chuckled. "Who's going to stop me?"

"I am," she said, her shoes sloshing as she tried to chase after him. Her clothes clung to her body, the T-shirt displaying the tantalizing thrust of her hardened nipples, her white shorts practically transparent. Todd's breath caught in his throat and his step faltered. She took full advantage of the hesitation to put both hands on his chest and shove. He stumbled backward, but caught himself just in time to prevent himself from tumbling backwards off the dock.

"You'd better be very glad that didn't work," he said softly. He shot her a look of feigned menace.

The spark in her eyes dimmed. "Oh?" she taunted right back.

"Between us I have the only dry clothes," he pointed out. "Not that I'm complaining about the way you look in those, you understand, but they are a bit provocative."

Her gaze lowered self-consciously and her cheeks flushed pink. "If you were a gentleman, you'd do something."

"Already we have a problem," he teased with a wicked grin.

"Todd, don't you have a beach towel in the car?"

"I might."

"Well, then, get it," she said. He had a feeling she was only barely resisting the urge to stamp her foot in annoyance.

Reluctantly, he went to the car and got her a towel. When he came back, he'd also taken off his shirt. He held both items out to her. Her gaze seemed riveted to his bare chest.

"Liz."

"Umm..."

"Your towel. My shirt. Don't you want to go inside and dry off?"

She still looked slightly dazed, a fact he found more than a little flattering, to say nothing of arousing. Of all the times and places to stir her senses—and his own. Shirt and towel slid from his fingers as he stepped closer. Her gaze held by his, Liz waited. She ran her tongue across her lips and his heart thudded. The woman's power to arouse him awed him. Her ability to do it at the most inconvenient times was just part of what made her fascinating.

Before he could enfold her in his arms, he heard Kevin's shout, then the thunder of feet along the dock.

"Hey, Dad, guess what. I have 'lexia. Ann says she knows just what that is. And you know what else, Dad? She says I'm going to get to swim with the dolphins. Isn't that great? Wait till the kids in school hear about it."

He skidded to a stop and his expression changed from excitement to bemusement as he saw Liz dripping from head to toe. "Mrs. Gentry, what happened? You're all wet."

"It seems Mrs. Gentry couldn't wait for you. She's already been for a swim with the dolphins."

"In her clothes?"

Todd grinned, ignoring her murderous glance. "Like I said, son, she couldn't wait."

Ann arrived just in time to hear the tail end of the conversation. Her eyebrows rose questioningly and her lips twitched with amusement. "I don't suppose I need to ask how this happened."

Liz grimaced. "A friend would not gloat. A friend would get me some dry clothes."

"I brought you a towel and offered you my shirt," Todd countered indignantly.

"I wanted something dry," she retorted, staring pointedly at the shirt and towel in question. They were floating in the water. As they watched, one of the other dolphins approached the shirt cautiously and, after a brief investigation, swam off with it.

"That's Jacquie," Ann said. "She's the most curious of any of our dolphins."

"Terrific," Todd muttered, though he couldn't resist laughing at the dolphin's antics. Jacquie seemed as pleased with her new acquisition as any other lady who'd been on an unscheduled shopping trip and had found a bargain in a favorite color.

"Why don't you two drive over to my place and scavenge around for some dry clothes," Ann suggested. "I've promised Kevin a chance to swim with the dolphins. One of the trainers will be here in a minute to take him in."

"I'd like to stay and watch," Todd said, "That is, if you don't object."

"Of course not. Liz, what about you? My clothes will be too big, but you're welcome to whatever you can find."

"I think I'll wait, too. The sun's hot. With this breeze, I'll drip dry in no time."

Within minutes Kevin was in the water with the dolphins, who seemed delighted to have a human playmate. They tossed a ball with him. They let him hold onto a fin, while they swam with him alongside. After each stunt, they waited for him to give them their reward. The excitement in Kevin's eyes made Todd's heart flip over. His laughter was young and carefree, exactly the way it should be for an eight-year-old and all too often hadn't been for Kevin.

When Ann finally called a halt to the swim, Kevin climbed out of the water reluctantly. "I get to do it again next week, right?" he begged Ann.

"You know the rules."

"I have to write an essay about what we did today."

"That's right. I want it to be the very best you can do, okay? You have a whole week to work on the spelling. I want you to do it all on your own. No help from your dad or Mrs. Gentry. You can have them look it over when you're finished, if you want to, but you write it by yourself. Try to tell me everything that happened."

Kevin threw his arms around Ann's waist with an impulsiveness that startled all of them. "I will. I promise."

All the way home Liz listened to Kevin's nonstop chattering. She felt warm inside, as if her mission had finally been accomplished. In time, Kevin would be okay. He would learn how to cope with his dyslexia, how to minimize its impact on his life.

This was what her life was all about—helping kids. This was something that really mattered. Getting involved with a man like Todd was only a risk, an unnecessary complication. She needed to extricate herself from the relationship before one of them got hurt. Already she was too attracted to him, already he was able to wound her far too easily. His irritation that morning, his obvious resentment of what he viewed as her interference had hurt. The more entangled their lives became, the greater the risk of emotional scars when the school year ended and Kevin no longer provided the link between them.

Lost in thought, she didn't notice until it was too late that Todd had driven to his place in Coconut Grove. Reluctantly she followed him inside as Kevin ran off to find paper and pencil so he could begin working on his essay about the dolphins. She glanced at Todd and caught the pride in his eyes. It filled her with satisfaction, knowing that she'd had a small part in their happiness.

"I've never seen him this carefree, this anxious to do any sort of homework," Todd said. "Thank you for giving him this chance."

"You're giving him the chance. I just pointed you in the right direction."

"I'm still not sure I understand the connection between the dolphins and Kevin's dyslexia."

"They're the incentive. They give Kevin a reason to succeed with the actual reading and writing exercises. He wants to swim with them again and by having him describe the experience, Ann is getting him to take auditory and visual experiences and put them down on paper. I'm not sure I understand why it works. I only know it does. I don't suppose it would have to be dolphins. It could be anything a child really loves, something that will make the struggle to put words on paper worthwhile."

"However it works, I'm grateful."

Just then Kevin came racing back to join them. He was waving a sheet of notebook paper. "Hey, Dad, look at this. What do you think?"

"You've finished your essay already?"

"Yeah. I wrote all about swimming with the dolphin and I said that you and Mrs. Gentry were there, too. Look at it. How'd I do?"

"Remember what Dr. Davies said, you're supposed to do this on your own."

"But she said I could let you look at it."

"Not right now, son. Mrs. Gentry and I were talking."

Liz couldn't believe he was putting such a damper on Kevin's excitement. She held out her hand. "Bring it here, Kevin. I'd like to see it."

Kevin gave his father one last disappointed look before bringing the paper to her. He handed it to her solemnly. "This is very well written, Kevin. Maybe you could try to put in a little more about what you did with the dolphins in the water."

"You mean like playing catch with them?"

"Exactly. And be sure to double-check your spelling."

He grinned. "I'll bet that means I made a mistake somewhere, huh?"

"Just a couple. You can figure them out."

"Okay. Thanks." He bounded off, his enthusiasm renewed.

Liz turned to Todd. "Why wouldn't you at least look at his paper?"

"Ann didn't want him to have help."

"That wasn't help. It was support. He was excited. He just wanted to share it."

"Then I was wrong. Can we get back to us for a minute?"

He reached out to take her in his arms, but she backed away a step. "I think I should go."

"Because of what just happened?"

"Of course not. I just don't think this is a good idea."

"Please change your mind, Liz. Stay here tonight. Don't make me take you home just yet. Help Kevin and me celebrate his first lesson at Dolphin Reach."

Her breath caught in her throat. Longing swept through her, followed by determination. She could see right through his manipulation. She couldn't allow him to use Kevin to hold her. "I can't," she insisted.

Todd frowned. "Can't or won't?" he asked, obviously puzzled.

"Does it really matter?"

"Liz, what's going on here? I thought we were going to try to move ahead, take this relationship one day at a time and see where it went."

She shook her head. "I tried to make you understand. I don't have relationships. Not the kind you mean. I know how I want to spend the rest of my life. I want to teach. I want to have a few good friends, people I can count on."

"And you don't think you'll be able to count on me?"

"You and I aren't friends, Todd. We're physically attracted. We have a common bond through Kevin. That doesn't add up to friendship."

He looked as though she'd struck him. "Is that how you view the last couple of weeks? A couple of parent-teacher conferences and a few passionate kisses?"

"That's exactly what it's been," she said stubbornly.

"I see. Then I'm the one who's had it all wrong. I thought the feelings ran a little deeper. Forgive me. It's been so long since I've wanted to hold anyone in my arms, I thought it must mean something."

She winced at his demeaning tone. "I didn't mean to make it sound cheap. I'm sorry. I'm not very good at this."

"Neither am I, apparently," he said dryly. She sensed that he was struggling with his temper. She honestly couldn't blame him. She'd been sending mixed signals. That was all the more reason to clarify things now.

Todd wasn't waiting for a response from her, though. "So," he said with an attempt to sound casual, "what say we start over? Let's try to become friends."

She blinked. This wasn't what she'd expected, at all. She'd anticipated anger, reproach, but not this cool acceptance, this rational proposition.

He grinned. "Not what you were expecting, huh?"

"Not exactly."

"Look, I'm willing to admit that maybe everything has happened too fast. Rather than turning our backs on it though, why not start over and go about this more slowly, just get to be friends. You say you want friends you can count on. I'd like to be one."

Liz was filled with doubts. A man like Todd as a friend? Impossible. "Do you honestly think we can put limits on this?"

"We can try."

Todd watched the play of emotions on her face and held his breath. He knew this was the only way he was likely to keep Liz in his life. Unless he could persuade her that staying was safe, she would run from the more intense emotions. Quite possibly it was the only time in his life, he'd deliberately set out to turn his life into a living hell. He had no doubt that's what it would be, too. Having Liz close enough to touch, but off-limits would be sheer torment.

He watched her reaction closely. She seemed perplexed by the offer, doubtful of his sincerity. More than that, though, she seemed tempted. That alone told him that given time, he might just be able to pass through hell to get to heaven.

Chapter Ten

For nearly three weeks, Liz and Todd struggled valiantly to maintain a purely platonic relationship. The vow to retreat from the intensity and get to know each other hovered over them, keeping their desires in check but not entirely forgotten.

They talked nightly on the phone, even when they'd parted barely an hour earlier. Sometimes the conversations were no more than a quick goodnight, a hurried reminder of the next day's plans. Sometimes they lasted for hours.

Todd tried to schedule every spare minute, insisting that the outings were just casual.

"It's not a date," he'd say in the midst of Liz's increasingly weak objections. "We're just going to a movie."

Or they'd go fishing, or to a football game, or to whatever he'd dreamed up to bring them together. He made each invitation seem so innocent, so persuasive that to refuse seemed churlish.

Besides, Liz told herself, they were just having fun. It had been a long time since she'd had a pal who enjoyed doing impulsive, spur-of-the-moment things. She and Todd were increasingly comfortable together. She was almost able to ignore the little zing that shot through her when his hand brushed her accidentally. She was certain that with a little more practice, she'd stop gazing at his lips and remembering them hard and seductive against hers.

She told herself it was all a question of mind over matter. If she concentrated hard enough on what they were doing, she'd forget all about what they *weren't* doing. It rarely worked.

They went to the movies, left halfway through and picked up a 1940s comedy at the video store. Sitting side by side on the sofa, a huge bowl of buttered popcorn between them, their hands repeatedly touched until Liz, feeling increasingly desperate, finally stopped reaching for more.

They went fishing. Todd caught several red snapper. Liz got sunburned because she hadn't been able to bring herself to ask Todd to spread lotion across her back. Simply touching his shoulders with the cool sunscreen had set her on fire. The thought of his hands on her, even in the most innocent caress, had left her weak and trembling.

Todd called in a few favors to get tickets for the hottest game on the University of Miami's football schedule. Despite the noisy crowd in the Orange Bowl, Liz fell asleep during halftime, exhausted from night after night of restless tossing and turning to avoid dreams that seemed filled with Todd.

They took Kevin to Metrozoo, where Liz claimed to be so enchanted by the aviary that she spent the entire day there. She'd been unable to face the fact that she was growing increasingly attached to the two of them, that every excursion felt more like a family outing, the kind she'd envisioned with Ed and Laura and never really had. She was losing her heart and had no idea how to go about reclaiming it.

They walked in the Grove at dusk, ate Mexican food on the terrace at Señor Frog's, then strolled a few blocks down Main Highway to have frozen yogurt for dessert. Her own yogurt melted and ran down her arm, when she got lost in the sight of Todd's tongue slowly licking the swirl of chocolate and vanilla.

Back at his place, he dragged out a guitar and strummed along to album after album of Bob Dylan songs, beginning and ending with 'Lay, Lady, Lay.' All Liz could think about was how it would feel to have those blunt, calloused fingers stroking her flesh with the same gentle touch as she lay across her own brass bed.

It was exactly the sort of nondemanding, friendly relationship Liz had been so sure she wanted. It was driving her crazy.

There were nights when Todd left her house that she paced the floor until three in the morning trying to figure out why he no longer kissed her goodnight. The fact that she'd set the rules only irritated her. There were days in her classroom, when she caught herself staring at Kevin and wondering what a child of hers and Todd's would look like. There were moments in the supermarket, when she found herself automatically buying food enough for three instead of one.

On rare occasions, usually in the middle of sleepless nights, she admitted to herself she was hooked. Not once, though, did she call it love. She knew perfectly well it was a silly obsession. Denial was a potent aphrodisiac. She actually considered abandoning the stupid rules and trying to seduce him, but figured she didn't know the first thing about how to do it. If he merely laughed at her, if he'd lost interest, she would die of embarrassment.

When she actually stopped to think about the amount of time she was wasting daydreaming about her relationship with Todd—or the lack of one—she wondered if perhaps she ought to go into counseling. He wasn't turning his life inside out over this. He'd amiably accepted the restrictions and gone on about his business.

His shopping mall was still on schedule. In fact he and Hank were already in negotiations to build another one. He'd taken her to the top of the parking garage to get a view of this one at night with all the lights on and the fountains glistening. She'd never thought of a shopping mall—much less a parking garage—as romantic. Todd's was.

There were no puffy, dark circles under his eyes from sleepless nights, as there were beneath hers. When she'd grumpily asked how he'd been sleeping, he'd said cheerfully, "Never better." She believed him. If anything, he looked healthier and seemed happier than he had when she'd first met him.

She couldn't even goad him into an argument. She found she missed the arguments almost as much as she missed his kisses.

"This isn't working," she announced that night as she prepared dinner for the three of them at his place.

He glanced up from the blueprint he was studying at the kitchen counter. "What's wrong with it? It smells great."

She snatched the blueprint away and tossed it across the room. "I am not talking about dinner!"

"Okay," he said cautiously. "What's the problem?"

"I am not your housekeeper."

"I never suggested that you were."

"Then why am I over here every night cooking dinner?"

"We could come to your place, if that would be easier," he offered cheerfully.

She threw a plate across the room and watched in fascinated horror as it shattered. She *never* threw things. She discussed things in a quiet, rational tone. At least she always had in the past.

"You idiot," she shouted. "You are missing the point." She picked up another plate. He caught her wrist.

"If you throw any more, we'll *have* to eat at your place. I'll be out of dishes. Care to tell me what this is really about."

"It's about us. I've known you barely a month and you're already taking me for granted."

"Liz, I do not take you for granted. I appreciate all the time we spend together. We have a lot of fun. You're a great cook."

"See what I mean. Who cares if I'm a great cook?"

"You were the one who said you didn't want to go out to dinner so much, that you enjoyed cooking."

"Would you get that pea-brain of yours away from your stomach and think about us for a minute."

"Us?"

"Yes, us. You're not exactly courting me anymore."

"Courting you? Correct me if I'm wrong, but didn't you tell me that you had no intention of ever becoming involved in another relationship? Didn't we agree to just be friends?"

"Yes, but..."

"Are you telling me you've changed your mind?" There was a gleam of satisfaction in his eyes when he said it. She barely noticed. She was too intent on expressing the rage that had been building for days now.

"No. Yes. Dammit, Todd, I can't even think with you around."

"I'd leave," he said reasonably, "but it's my place."

"Then I'll go."

To her astonishment and absolute fury, he didn't try to stop her. He did call her at midnight to whisper goodnight. He was definitely trying to drive her crazy.

Two days after Liz had stalked out of his kitchen in a huff, Todd was bent over a sheet of figures on cost overruns when Kevin came to stand beside him.

"Can it wait, son?" he asked, fighting as always to make sure the numbers were being correctly interpreted by his mind. He had less trouble with math than he did with reading, but he still didn't trust himself. A distraction was the last thing he needed.

"Sure. I guess so," Kevin said, but didn't move.

Todd glanced at him and pushed aside the papers. "Why do I have the feeling I'd better listen now? Is everything okay?"

Kevin shifted uneasily from foot to foot. "I did something in school today. I think maybe you're going to be mad about it."

Todd's heart sank. From the reports he'd gotten from Liz lately, he'd thought Kevin's days of troublemaking were behind him. "Go on."

"I volunteered you for something."

Cautious relief eased through him. "What exactly did you volunteer me for?"

"I said you'd be one of our room mothers," Kevin blurted, watching him warily.

Todd's eyebrows shot up at that.

"I mean I know you'd be a room father, but that's not what they call them. Will you do it?"

"What exactly does a room *mother* do?"

"Helps with parties and field trips and stuff."

"For the whole year?"

"Yeah. The kids all think it'll be really neat to have a father do it for a change."

Todd sensed that the real issue had been Kevin's desperate desire to be like the other kids. He didn't have a mother to offer up for service, so he'd presented his father as the logical alternative.

Todd found he was torn between annoyance and delight. "Is there something special coming up that will require my presence? You know I have to plan ahead if I'm going to be away from work."

Kevin's face lit up. "Then you'll do it? You'll really do it?" He was practically bouncing up and down in his excitement. Todd felt his heart flip over. How much had Sarah's abandonment cost his son? Would he be able to make up for all the big things as easily as he'd made up for this little one?

"I'll do it," he promised. Even if he would feel like a damned fool. Room mother, indeed. Liz had probably been chuckling all afternoon. "I'll call Mrs. Gentry and work out the details."

"Great, Dad," Kevin said, throwing his arms around his neck and hugging him tightly. A lump of unexpected emotion lodged in Todd's throat.

"Dad, can I ask you something?"

"Of course."

"Are you and Mrs. Gentry gonna get married?"

Todd swallowed hard. Out of the mouths of babes... "Son, where would you get an idea like that?"

"You see her all the time and I even saw you kiss her once. I figured maybe you were going to get married."

"And how would you feel if we did?"

Kevin shrugged. "It'd be neat, I guess. I haven't had a mom in a long time. I think she'd be a pretty good one to have. She takes real good care of us."

"Well, son, I don't know if you can understand this, but I do like Mrs. Gentry a whole lot. I'm just not so sure we're ready to start talking about marriage."

"Oh," Kevin said, looking more disappointed than Todd had anticipated.

"I'll make you a promise, though. If things change, you'll be the first to know."

"Okay, Dad. Thanks for being room mother," he said and bounded off to share the news with one of his friends.

Todd sat for a long time afterwards staring into space. Marriage, huh? He couldn't deny that the thought had crossed his mind with increasing frequency. Had Liz thought about it? Was that why she'd been so touchy lately? Had this crazy game they'd been playing finally forced her to acknowledge her feelings? He'd thought the other night that she was beginning to come around. The clatter of broken plates had actually warmed his heart. If she didn't actually admit to a change in her way of thinking of them soon, he might very well have to resort to more aggressive tactics to remind her of exactly how terrific they were in each other's arms.

With that resolution in mind, he picked up the phone and called her. As always, just the sound of her voice improved his mood. "Okay, lady, what's this room-mother stuff?"

Her low chuckle sent flames leaping through him. "I thought you'd be thrilled. Not every child is so enthused about having a parent do the job. Kevin can hardly wait."

"So I gathered. Do I have to wear an apron?"

"I think you can probably skip the apron, though you looked pretty cute in the one you wore to barbecue the chicken the night Hank and Gina came over."

"When's my first assignment?"

"Ahh, I see Kevin left the dirty work to me."

"Uh-oh. I don't think I'm going to like this."

"Oh, I don't know. How do you feel about baking cookies?"

"Baking cookies?" he asked in a slightly horrified whisper. Chicken on the grill was the height of his culinary expertise.

"Little pumpkins would be nice," Liz continued, amusement lacing through her voice. "It should be fairly simple for a man of your exceptional talents. Maybe round sugar cookies with orange icing and cute little faces drawn on them. What do you think?"

"I think you and my son have lost your minds. I have never baked a cookie in my life. I'll pick some up at the bakery."

"Store-bought cookies are not the same," Liz chided. "Especially for Halloween. Ask any third-grader."

"Then you can plan on getting your cute little tush over here to help me."

"Is that any way to talk to your son's teacher?" she inquired with feigned indignation. He heard quite clearly her stifled laughter.

"When do you want the cookies?"

"The Halloween party is next Friday, after lunch." Her tone turned serious. "Really, Todd, will this be okay for you? I know you have work to do."

"It's important to Kevin. I'll make it okay. As for you, we have a date for Thursday night to bake cookies."

"Should be interesting," she said, which he assumed was an acceptance. It was also an incredible understatement. If he had his way, the night would involve more than browning a few cookies in the oven.

"By the way," he added idly, "if you ever tell Hank about this, I will show your coworkers the pictures of you being dunked by a dolphin." He hung up on her sputtered protest.

When Liz showed up at Todd's the following Thursday at seven, she found him with flour up to his elbows and sprinkled across his nose. She brushed it away and gave him a quick kiss. A *friendly* kiss. She stiffened her spine resolutely and marched past him. "Any flour left for the cookies?"

"You really are pressing your luck," he growled as he followed her back to the kitchen. She stood in the doorway and stared. All the starch went right out of her spine. There was a white dusting of flour everywhere and one suspicious looking glob on the floor. Todd apparently caught the direction of her gaze and muttered, "I dropped an egg."

"Looks more like the whole carton."

"Okay, so it was a couple of eggs."

She found the fact that he was throwing himself into the project with such abandon a little touching. For all his grumbling, she had a feeling he was enjoying the fact that Kevin had wanted him involved in his school activities. She hoped he also realized that it was another sign of Kevin's growing adaptation.

Looking around again at his enthusiastic efforts, she shook her head. She had a hunch she should have let him buy the cookies.

She dusted off a stool by the counter and sat down. "Since everything's obviously under control, I think I'll just watch awhile."

"Don't be sarcastic, sweetheart. Roll up your sleeves and get to work. I've already sifted the flour."

"Yes. I can see that."

He shot her a venomous look. She grinned and reached for the cookbook. "Let's see now. Two cups of sifted flour."

"I'm tripling the recipe."

"Good God!"

"Kids eat a lot of cookies, right? Besides we may lose a few until I get this right."

"Smart thinking."

"Thank you."

"Have you added the sugar?"

"Done."

"Butter?"

"Here."

"A kiss?"

His head shot up. She wondered where the devil that had come from. She tried for a nonchalant shrug. "Just wanted to be sure you were paying attention."

Before she realized what he intended, he moved around the counter, circled her waist with his arms and covered her mouth. There was no time to protest that she'd only been teasing. And there was nothing light-hearted about Todd's kiss. It was every bit as greedy and soul-shattering as the ones she'd recalled. The last of her cool resistance melted away, until she was warm and pliable in his arms. How had she survived the last few weeks of denial? When she was breathless and limp, he stepped back with a satisfied smirk.

"I think I like that ingredient the best."

"Oh, yes," she whispered, her eyes locked with his. If she had her way this was just the first of many. They would overdose on kisses. They would drop the pretenses, go with the flow, whatever the current vernacular was for admitting that she couldn't go on a minute longer without knowing what it would be like to have Todd caress her and love her. It was several excruciating, timeless minutes later when she finally dragged her attention back to the recipe.

The first batch of cookies was finally in the oven. The rest were laid out on cookie sheets waiting. Todd poured them each a cup of coffee and sat down beside her at the counter. Liz held the warm mug in both hands and sipped slowly, not liking the unexpected direction of her thoughts. Why was there always this one part of her brain that insisted on being sensible? Why did sanity have to creep in, just when she was ready to experience the glory of giving in to temptation?

She tried very hard to tell her brain to mind its own damned business. Unfortunately, it didn't seem to be listening. The nagging thought was something she hadn't been able to shake ever since Kevin had volunteered his father to be room mother.

"Todd," she began finally.

"Oh, dear. I don't like the sound of this," he said.

"I haven't said anything yet."

"But you're going to, and that tone tells me it's not good news."

"It's not bad news exactly. It's just a question."

"Go on."

"Have you ever heard from Sarah?"

The look he turned on her was appalled. "Where did that come from?"

"I just wondered. You've never really said."

"No. The divorce was handled by our attorneys. She didn't contest it. I have no idea where she is."

That was good, she supposed. Or was it? She took a deep breath and reached over to put her hand on his. He turned his hand palm up and enfolded hers.

"What's going on in that head of yours?" he asked softly.

She lifted troubled eyes to his. "Do you think maybe you should try to find her?"

He released her hand and stood up so fast the stool went spinning and crashed into the counter. "Are you out of your mind?" he exploded. "Why would I want to do that?"

"For Kevin's sake," she said simply, then went on with a rush before he could snap her head off. "Maybe he needs to know his mother. Not live with her or anything like that. Just get to know her."

"You seem to be forgetting one little thing: Sarah wanted nothing to do with Kevin."

"It's been a long time. Maybe she misses him. Maybe she's sorry she left."

"She knows where to find us."

"Todd, don't let your pride stand in the way of what might be best for Kevin."

"How can knowing a self-involved, uncaring woman like Sarah possibly be best for him?"

"She's his mother," she repeated staunchly. "He has a right to find out about her for himself."

"When he's older, I won't try to stop him. But now? No way. It would just be asking for more heartache. What the hell put this idea into your head? Was it this room-mother nonsense?"

"I guess so. It just seemed as though he wanted so badly to be like all the other kids."

Todd looked crushed. He stalked over to the oven and yanked out the trays of cookies, replacing them with the next batch. Liz waited. She could see the agony of indecision etched on his face. When he came back, he pulled her into his arms and held her close, his face buried in her hair. She could feel the steady rhythm of his heartbeat and knew that, in the end, his strength would bring him to the right decision.

"I'll think about it, okay?"

"That's all I can possibly ask."

He put a finger under her chin and tilted her head until he could look straight into her eyes. "Is this by any chance the last big barrier between us?"

She took a deep breath and nodded. "I think maybe it is."

"You don't make it easy for a guy, you know that, don't you?"

"That goes both ways. You've turned my life upside down, too."

His arms tightened around her. "God, I love you."

"Don't say that," she pleaded, but the words sang in her heart.

"She wants me to hunt for Sarah," Todd told Hank the next morning. "Can you imagine? I told her it's the worst idea I've ever heard, but she's got this crazy notion that Kevin needs his mother."

"Maybe she's right," Hank said, not looking up from the blueprints spread across the desktop.

Todd crumpled the soda can in his hand and threw it across the room. "Not you, too! Is everyone around me going crazy at once?" The can hit the wall and toppled neatly into the trash can.

"Nice shot," Hank said. "It's not such a crazy idea and not just for Kevin's sake, either. Seems to me like a meeting with your ex might put a lot of ghosts to rest, once and for all."

"I am not living with any blasted ghosts!"

"Aren't you? You've been mooning around here over Liz for weeks now. If you ask me, the only reason you haven't asked her to marry you is because you're still scared to death that she'll dump you the way that Sarah did."

"Okay. I admit it. I'm scared. That's because Liz hasn't wanted anything more from me. She put up the barriers. It doesn't have anything to do with ghosts or living in the past."

"It does from where I sit. For some reason you're equating Liz with that creature who walked out on you. She may even sense that. Women have a way of trying to protect themselves when they see pain lurking on the horizon. If you ask me, she's been pretty smart to keep her distance. Deep down, you've always believed that every woman is just as shallow as Sarah."

"Liz is not like that."

"I believe that. I don't think you do."

"Dammit, where do you get off telling me what I believe?"

"Hey, you brought this up. I'll just ask one more thing and then I'll butt out. Have you told her about your dyslexia?"

He colored guiltily. "What does that have to do with anything?"

Hank shook his head at the blatant evasion. "You know the answer to that one, pal. Think about it."

Todd did little else the rest of the day. He didn't like the answer that kept coming up.

Chapter Eleven

A holiday party always seemed to bring out the worst in Liz's students. As excitement mounted, it was more and more difficult to keep their attention on their lessons. Even though she tried to keep their interest by devising holiday themes for their assignments, by lunchtime they were virtually out of control.

Losing patience finally, she stood at the front of the classroom and said very softly and emphatically, "If I don't have quiet in here by the time I count to five, there will be no party."

A stunned hush promptly fell over the room.

She nodded. "That's better. Now until our parents get here, I want you to write an essay describing your Halloween costume and why you chose it. There will be a prize for the best essay. Any questions?"

She looked around and saw that notebooks were being hurriedly opened. No hands went up. "Okay. You'll have about twenty minutes."

As she finished giving the instructions, she turned and saw Todd watching her from the doorway. He'd dressed in western garb, complete with red bandanna at his neck, cowboy boots and a hat that looked as though it had served an extended tour of duty on a dusty, lonesome trail. The outfit suited him. Her heart thumped unsteadily as she went to join him. She had an unexpected longing to desert this classroom and head west with him before sundown. An image of cool Montana nights and the glow of camp fires held an undeniable appeal to a heart that had never before yearned to roam.

"Howdy, pardner," she teased in a voice that was surprisingly steady. "I like the duds."

"You look a mite fancy for a place like this," he observed with a pretty fair imitation of a Texas twang. "In fact, you look as though you ought to be sipping mint juleps with Scarlet and Rhett."

She brushed a hand over the wide hoop skirt that suddenly made her feel delicate and feminine next to his blatant virility. "It's a little much, but it was all the costume shop had left in my size, unless I wanted to come as a robot."

His eyes blazed approvingly. "This is a definite improvement over clinking metal. I like skirts that swish. As for that neckline..."

Liz felt the heat rise in her cheeks. She'd known that darn neckline was too revealing. She'd figured no third-grader would notice. She hadn't stopped to consider how Todd would react. Or had she?

"Did you bring everything in or do you need to go back to the car?" she said.

He grinned wickedly at her nervous change of subject. "Okay, Miss Liz, but we'll get back to that neckline later. I have the cookies and the punch mix here."

"Then you might as well start setting up. It'll give the kids hope that this party is actually going to happen."

When they'd put the trays of cookies on a table set up in the back of the room, he leaned down to whisper, "I don't suppose it would be proper for the teacher to get caught being kissed by the room mother."

"Good deduction," she said as her pulse zipped along.

"So what do we do to kill time until we start this shindig?"

Forcing herself to be matter-of-fact when her thoughts kept zooming back to the last time Todd had been in her classroom, she said, "I've put out the punch bowl. You can start mixing the juice and ginger ale. Jamey's mother should be here in a minute. She's bringing the cups, plates and napkins. Once everything's ready, we'll have the costume parade. You two get to be the judges. The principal will be the third judge."

"Are there criteria?"

"Scariest and most unusual."

"Are Jamey and Kevin disqualified? I may be biased, but I do think my son looks especially handsome in his Indy 500 jumpsuit."

"He still can't get your vote. He and Jamey get extra cookies for giving up the right to compete."

"I suppose that's fair. I'd go for the cookies myself, if I hadn't been the one who baked them. After you left last night, I must have tried one from every batch just to be sure they tasted okay. I've decided that a sugar binge is every bit as deadly as drinking alcohol. My stomach still rolls over at the sight of all that orange goo." He shuddered convincingly.

"That is not goo," Liz protested. "It's frosting. Admittedly, they may not look much like pumpkins, but they're just fine. The kids will love them."

"Hey, you're the one who drew the faces on them. Don't blame me if they look weird."

When they'd finished making the punch, Todd's expression turned serious. "Do we have time to talk before the party gets rolling?"

Liz glanced around the room. "If you can talk fast. Chaos tends to erupt without notice."

"I've been thinking about what you said last night."

Her head snapped up at that. Her hands stilled over the trays of cookies. "About Sarah?"

"Yes. I talked to Hank about it, too. He agrees that maybe it's time to try to find her, for my sake as much as Kevin's."

Liz felt her heart begin to thud. That wasn't something she'd considered when she'd made the suggestion. She hadn't been thinking of Todd, at all, only

Kevin. "I'm not sure I understand," she said uneasily.

He touched her lips with the tip of his finger. "No frowns, sweetheart. Hank thinks maybe I've let the memories of the past ruin the future for me. He thinks seeing Sarah will put them to rest."

"Do you agree?"

"Not entirely, but I'm willing to look for her for Kevin's sake, anyway. I think you're both right about that. I talked to a detective before I came over here."

"What did he say?"

"That it could take awhile, that I shouldn't get my hopes up, that people who want to vanish generally cover their tracks pretty well, especially when they've had a four-year head start."

"For what it's worth, I think you're doing the right thing," she said, though her voice shook. She couldn't quite bring herself to meet his gaze. She was afraid of what she'd see there. Was he beginning to anticipate seeing Sarah after all this time? How much claim did his ex-wife still have on his heart? For her to have had the power to hurt him so badly, he must have loved her very much.

"Your opinion is worth a lot," he said, tilting her chin up until she had to face him. "I know how much you care about Kevin. That's the reason I'm doing this. The only reason."

Still filled with doubts despite the reassurance, she nodded and abruptly turned to go back to the front of the room.

"Liz."

She looked back.

"Don't say anything to Kevin. If we find Sarah, I want to talk to her first, see where she's coming from before I tell him about this. I don't want him hurt again."

"I understand. This is something between you and your son, Todd. It has nothing to do with me." She wanted so badly to be brave, to face the possibility that this could cost her everything. Instead, her tone simply came out clipped and icy.

He sighed, no doubt understandably confused by what he must view as her sudden change of heart. "You're wrong, Liz. It has everything to do with you. Because of you, Kevin may have his mother back in his life and you and I may be able to move on with our life."

Todd's words were nothing more than an empty promise, she kept telling herself as despair wrapped itself around her. Ed had solemnly repeated the wedding vows and, in the end, they'd meant nothing.

Worried and trying not to let it spoil the party for the kids, she went to help them begin getting into their Halloween costumes. Never in her life had she been more thankful of the noisy distraction of thirty-five high-spirited eight-year-olds. Never had she been more in need of those shy smiles and exuberant hugs. She felt as if her entire life was suddenly hanging in the balance. She'd never expected to feel that way again. She hadn't wanted to let any man get that close. Now it looked as though her worst fears were coming true. She was dangerously close to losing the man she loved.

* * *

It was nearly a month before Todd heard from the detective he'd hired. On the Monday before Thanksgiving, Laurence Patterson called with the news that he'd found Sarah. She was living in a small town in the Florida Panhandle. She was working as a hostess in a restaurant at a resort hotel on the Gulf coast. She'd never remarried, though there was apparently an older man with whom she'd been involved for the past year.

"I have a picture I can send you. Do you want me to talk to her or do you plan to take it from here?" Patterson asked.

Todd wanted the whole thing to go away. He'd almost convinced himself that the search was going to turn up no news and that he and Kevin would go on with their lives just as they had been for the last four years. He would convince Liz to marry him and they would all live happily ever after. The easiest thing would have been to ask for the picture, pay the detective for his time and pretend that it had all been a dead end. He had seen Liz's doubts magnified out of all proportion over the last few weeks. He could put them to rest once and for all by not involving Sarah in their lives.

But he knew he'd never be able to look either Liz or Kevin in the eyes again, if he told the lie.

"Send the picture and your bill, but I'll take it from here. Do you have a phone number and address for her?"

Patterson gave him the information, including her schedule at work. When he'd hung up, Todd turned around and stared out the window at the tropical setting he'd created in his backyard. Today it didn't have the power to soothe him. He wanted Liz. He needed her sensible advice, her gentle smile and the love that radiated from her, even as she protested that she didn't believe in the emotion. He knew, though, that he was on his own with this one. He had to make the decision, plan how he would handle the meeting. He had to live with it. Then he had to convince Liz that they were going to be just fine.

He glanced at the picture of Kevin on his desk and made up his mind. He called his travel agent and booked a flight for the next day. Putting it off would only make the prospect loom larger.

At noon Tuesday, his heart hammering, he walked through the bright, airy lobby of the Sea Tide Inn and through the French doors leading to the restaurant.

He saw Sarah before she saw him. Reed slender, blond and elegant, she was seating a family of six at a large, round table that overlooked the Gulf of Mexico. She was friendly, which didn't surprise him. She'd always been a wonderful hostess. What amazed him was that she was thoroughly at ease with the kids. She actually seemed to be enjoying their teasing boisterousness.

It was only when she came back to her hostess station and caught sight of him that her smile faded. Her eyes widened in shock. Her step faltered. She tried a tentative smile, but couldn't maintain it.

"Hello, Sarah," he said quietly. To his astonishment there was no anger underlying the greeting. In

place of love-turned-to-hate, there was only emptiness. So many years of wasted energy, he thought with
regret. At least he would be able to return to Liz at
peace, knowing that the love he felt for her was whole,
untainted by the past.

"Todd, what are you doing here?" She sounded
more curious than dismayed.

He smiled faintly. "Frankly, I'm a little surprised
myself."

"Then this is a coincidence?"

"No. As a matter of fact, I hired a detective to look
for you."

The color drained from her face. "Why? Nothing's wrong, is it? Kevin..."

"He's fine. Do you have time to talk?"

"Actually, no," she said, then looked around,
clearly distraught. "Maybe I could find someone..."

"No. It's not necessary, really. This can wait."

"Are you sure? Could you come back about two? I
should be able to take a break by then."

He nodded. "I'll be back." He touched her hand in
a brief gesture of reassurance. "Don't worry, Sarah. I
promise everything's okay."

He spent the next two hours driving around the
area, trying to understand his initial reaction to this
meeting, which had been such a long time coming.
He'd realized at once that Sarah no longer mattered to
him, that her decision to go might very well have freed
him from a relationship that had been all wrong from
the first. At the time he'd been too caught up in the
rejection, too furious at the apparent ease of her

abandonment of Kevin to think clearly about the wisdom of what she was doing.

By the time he went back to the inn, he was in control of his emotions, looking forward to a final resolution. She was waiting for him, watching the door anxiously. Her expression brightened when she saw him.

"I thought we could have some lunch here, if that's okay with you," she said. "Even though the worst of the rush is over, I'm technically still on duty. I'll be able to keep an eye on things."

"No problem."

They settled at a comfortable table and ordered lunch. The waiter and busboy both treated Sarah with deference and she was genuinely kind to them.

"You seem to have found a niche for yourself here," he observed.

"I like it. The owners are wonderful people, the staff is great and I enjoy meeting so many tourists."

"Is it what you expected to find, when you left us?"

"Not exactly, but I'm content. I've grown up a lot in the last four years." She stirred her coffee, though she'd put nothing in it. It was the only hint now of her continued nervousness.

"How is Kevin really? You're sure everything's okay?" she asked finally.

"I'm surprised you're interested." He regretted the bitterness the minute he'd made the remark. He hadn't come to make accusations, only to move ahead.

She turned sad blue eyes on him. "I've always been interested, Todd. I just figured I'd given up the right to ask. I thought you both deserved a clean break. It was all I had to give you."

He hadn't counted on her still hurting. She was the one who'd walked away. He'd expected her to be carefree. "I'm sorry. I didn't mean to make this difficult for you. Kevin really is fine. I brought along some snapshots. Would you like to see them?"

There was a touching eagerness in her expression as she took the photos and went through them slowly, asking questions about where they'd been taken, how old he'd been.

"He's grown so much," she said with a sigh, when she'd looked at the last of them. She continued to hold them, running her fingers idly across the surface of the top photo as if she were caressing her son. She couldn't seem to drag her gaze away.

"Kids have a way of doing that. It seems every time I turn around, he's outgrown the clothes I bought."

"He's in school now?"

Todd nodded. "Third grade."

"How's he doing?"

"He's had some problems," he admitted reluctantly.

She frowned and put the snapshots back in front of him. "What sort of problems?"

"Behavior problems, at least that's what first got my attention. It seems you weren't the only one who thought he was unmanageable. His teacher this year finally forced the issue. We've had Kevin tested. He's dyslexic, just like me. A lot of his anger was caused by frustration. He's getting help now and things are better. Not perfect, but better.''

"I'm glad he's getting help."

"And I'm sorry I didn't listen to you. It might have saved him some rough times. It might have made a difference for all of us."

"Don't blame yourself. Neither of us was very good at communicating back then. I was better at yelling and running. You just wanted to stick that stubborn head of yours in the sand."

"You're not the first person lately to point out that my obstinacy gets me in trouble," he said with a rueful grin. He hesitated. "Sarah, do you want to come back?"

At her stunned expression, he said quickly. "I don't mean to stay. Just to see Kevin again. I think knowing that his mother still loves him might make a big difference in his life. This isn't an impulsive decision. I've been thinking about it."

Tears spilled down her cheeks at the invitation and for once Todd felt something at the sight of them. He pitied her for all the wonderful years she'd lost with her child. "You really wouldn't object?" she said in a choked whisper. "You'd let me see him?"

"You could spend Thanksgiving with us," he said, praying that Liz would understand. "I know it's short notice, but somehow that seems like the perfect time for a family reunion."

She reached across the table and clasped his hand. "I'll never be able to thank you enough for doing this.

I know how badly I hurt you. I can imagine how difficult it must have been for you to come."

"I love our son," he said simply. "I had to come." He stood up then. "I'll make the arrangements and get back to you, Sarah."

He was almost out the door, when he found himself turning back. She was sitting right where he'd left her, following him with eyes still luminous with unshed tears. He'd left the snapshots on the table and she was holding them tightly.

"You won't disappoint him, will you?" he said.

She shook her head. "Never again, Todd. I promise."

Liz felt her world shift and tumble off kilter when Todd called to tell her that Sarah would be coming for Thanksgiving.

"You've seen her, then?" she said in an amazingly calm tone. A chill seemed to settle over her.

"Today. I flew up to the Panhandle this morning. I didn't tell you before I went because I wasn't sure what I'd find. Maybe I just needed to handle it on my own."

"If she's coming here, that must mean it went okay."

"She's changed, Liz. Or maybe I'm the one who's different. I don't know. She misses Kevin. I could tell. I showed her pictures and she cried. I had to ask her to come. You understand, don't you?"

"Of course, I understand. This is what I wanted, remember?" But she hadn't wanted this. Not on Thanksgiving. She had wanted the three of them to spend the holiday together, like a real family. It was exactly the sort of dream she'd warned herself against having. It was turning into a nightmare.

"... I thought we could pick her up at the airport together," Todd was saying.

"What?" she said incredulously, certain she'd misunderstood. "What are you talking about?"

"On Thursday morning, I thought you and I would pick her up. I want you to meet her before I take her to the house. I need you to help me prepare Kevin for this."

"You want me there?"

"Of course, I want you there. We'd planned the day. Hank's coming. That should help some. Not that he's crazy about Sarah, but he'll be supportive. I know it may seem a little awkward for everyone, but I think it's the best way to handle it for Kevin's sake."

For Kevin's sake. But dammit, what about for her sake? How was she supposed to cope with being the outsider at this little gathering?

"Liz, what's wrong?"

"Nothing."

"Don't tell me nothing. You're upset. I know I probably shouldn't have sprung this on you at the last minute, but I thought this was what you wanted."

"It was. It is. Oh, Todd, I'm sorry. I don't know what's gotten into me. I guess the reality has thrown me more than I expected it to. I'll be fine by Thursday."

She was not fine. She covered her fears by wearing a dress that she knew was one of Todd's favorites, by cooking a meal that included all the traditional Thanksgiving fare, by setting Todd's table so perfectly it could have been photographed for a gourmet food magazine.

At her insistence, they warned Kevin about the surprise visitor they were having. He turned very quiet at the news and retreated to his room.

"What do you suppose is going on in his head?" Todd asked worriedly. "Maybe this was a mistake."

"You're doing the right thing," Hank said, walking in on the end of the scene. "Of course, he's going to be a little taken aback. Give him some time for it to sink in. When Sarah gets here, it'll be up to her to win him over."

In the end Todd went to the airport alone, leaving Hank and Liz with Kevin.

"Nervous?" Hank asked as she kept poking her head in the oven to check the turkey.

She let the door slam shut and paced instead.

"You don't have a thing to worry about, you know."

"Who says I'm worried?"

"Sorry," he said, grinning. "It was just a guess. For the record, though, I've known Todd for a lot of years. I was around when Sarah made mincemeat out of his heart. He's never been happier than he's been since he met you."

She sighed and touched his hand. "Thanks for the vote of confidence." Then she resumed pacing.

"Don't mention it." He caught her wrist as she passed by him for the fourth time. "Can I make a suggestion?"

"Why not?"

"Todd will probably kill me for butting in like this, but let me stay here with Kevin tonight."

"Why would you want to do that?" she said, staring at him in confusion.

"So you and Todd can be alone. Go to your place. Go to a hotel. It doesn't matter, as long as you spend some time together. I think you'll have a lot of talking to do, once Sarah's gone."

Hank's words were innocent enough, but his implication was anything but. Liz's face flamed in embarrassment, but she felt tears clog her throat. In that instant she decided that Hank Riley had more sensitivity than anyone she'd ever met besides Ann.

"You're a fraud," she accused softly, giving him a watery smile.

"Oh?" His eyes twinkled with amusement.

"Don't even waste your time trying to deny it. I just hope I'm around when the right woman takes the time to get beyond that tough, lecherous facade of yours."

"It'll never happen."

"That's what they all say, right before they fall."

The reunion between Sarah and Kevin was every bit as awkward as Liz and Todd had anticipated. Kevin stared at his plate all through dinner, speaking only when spoken to and then only in monosyllables. He never once looked directly at his mother. He asked to be excused even before Liz served the pumpkin pie. Sarah looked as if she might cry.

"Give him time," Liz told her gently, surprised at the compassion she was feeling toward her. She'd wanted so badly to hate her, but she found that she couldn't.

"Liz is right," Todd concurred.

"I'm not so sure. I hurt him very badly. Maybe I don't have the right to even ask his forgiveness."

"Everyone has the right to ask forgiveness," Liz said. "Kevin needs to learn that forgiving and forgetting are part of growing up, too."

"You can come back tomorrow," Todd reminded her. "You have the whole weekend to try to get through to him."

After they'd called a cab to take Sarah to a nearby hotel, the three of them cleaned up the dishes, then Hank looked pointedly at Liz before making a discreet exit to play video games with Kevin.

"What was that all about?" Todd asked, staring after him. "Hank usually can't wait to go off on some date after one of these holiday celebrations. Family togetherness makes him nervous."

"He's planning to play matchmaker tonight."

"Matchmaker?"

"He's offered to stay here, so you and I can be alone."

Todd looked stunned. "He had no right," he said indignantly. "I'm sorry if he embarrassed you, Liz."

She put a hand on his arm. "He didn't embarrass me."

"He should never...what?"

She grinned, hoping her expression conveyed bold daring, rather than the jittery nervousness she was feeling. "I said he didn't embarrass me. I think he's right. I think it's way past time for us to have an entire night alone." She stood on tiptoe and wound her arms around Todd's neck. Her mouth met his in a slow, sensuous caress. "Am I getting through to you yet?"

"I'm not sure," he said with feigned puzzlement. "Could you try that again?"

"With pleasure."

It was several minutes before Todd broke free of the heated embrace. Breathing hard, he whispered, "I think we'd better leave now or we'll have a helluva time explaining to Kevin why we locked him and Hank in the bedroom."

Liz nodded with a sort of lazy contentment. "After you," she murmured, certain that she had never before felt anything to match the warm glow that had settled deep inside her.

Todd shook his head as he linked her arm through his. "Together, sweetheart. From now on, we do it all together."

Chapter Twelve

Halfway to her house, Liz suffered the onset of a terminal case of cold feet. If there had been any way short of declaring a medical emergency to get Todd to turn the car around, she would have done it. Todd was the right man, but this was the wrong night. Sarah's presence had triggered a decision that should have been made under less volatile circumstances. She wasn't really ready. She'd be ready in another year or two—or perhaps the next century, whenever they started handing out guarantees with relationships.

She glanced over at Todd. He looked thoroughly at ease. Confident. Though his full attention appeared to be on the busy road, a smile played about his lips. She wondered if she'd put it there, if some private anticipation of the night ahead was already giving him pleasure. Renewed panic promptly set her heart to pounding harder. As if he'd heard it, Todd turned toward her. His expression immediately grew troubled.

"Second thoughts already?"

"What are you, a mind reader?" she said lightly.

"It's hard to miss the signs. You're holding onto your purse as if you're anticipating a mugging at every intersection. If you bite your lower lip much harder, it'll be far too sore for me to kiss it the way I want to."

Powerful, sensual images suddenly captivated her. "The way you want to," she repeated weakly. She was going to faint, just from the caress of his words. One actual kiss and she would simply float happily into oblivion. She swallowed hard and tried to appear only mildly interested in the direction of the conversation.

Todd, however, was not through with the torment. In a voice that slid over her senses like silk, he said, "All I've been able to think about all day is a slow, leisurely kiss. There were too damned many people around. I wanted to taste your mouth when it was still flavored by cranberry sauce and wine. When you ate the whipped cream off your pumpkin pie, I could just imagine..."

Liz knew exactly what he could imagine. She wasn't sure she could stand hearing him say it, though. "Todd, do you think we could talk about something else?" Her own voice was no more than a husky whisper.

"Why? Is this bothering you?"

"No." The denial came out as a squeak. "It's just that there's a lot of traffic. You really ought to be paying attention. If you're thinking about kissing and . . . whatever else it is you're thinking about, you might be distracted. You know what the drivers are like around here. You have to drive defensively every second."

"I think you're the one who's distracted," he taunted, sounding very pleased about it.

"But you see that doesn't really matter," she insisted. "I'm not driving."

"Okay. I'll concentrate on driving, if you'll tell me what you're thinking about." There was a wicked boldness behind the suggestion. Liz's heart lurched once, then set off at an erratic clip that should have required installation of a pacemaker. "Well?"

She tried to stall for time to gather her thoughts. She needed to come up with a diversionary tactic that was far removed from the wildly sensual images that were actually rampaging through her mind.

"I, um, I was just wondering if I turned the dishwasher on before we left your house."

Weak, Elizabeth, she thought disgustedly. Really weak. She glanced over at Todd to see how he'd reacted. He was regarding her skeptically. Amusement danced in his eyes. "Oh, really?"

She persisted with dogged determination. "Maybe I should call Hank and check, when we get to my place. I'd hate to have all those dishes waiting for us tomorrow."

"I turned the dishwasher on."

"Oh."

"Anything more on your mind? Perhaps you'd like to discuss something a little less weighty? Perhaps a solution for world peace?"

She glared at him. "Don't make fun of me."

She caught him struggling with a grin. "I don't mean to, sweetheart. It's just that you're taking all this so seriously."

"It is serious."

"It's meaningful. It's wonderful. It is not life or death. Making love is a natural outgrowth of a relationship between a man and a woman. I want you, Liz. I've wanted you in my arms and in my bed practically since the first time I saw you."

"We're going to be in my bed," she pointed out irrationally.

Todd laughed. "Caught on a technicality. Want me to call Hank and have him take Kevin to his place for the night?"

"Don't be ridiculous."

"It's hard not to be, when you're acting like a giddy teenager who's afraid her parents are going to discover that she knows all about sex."

She immediately stiffened. "I'm sorry, if I can't be casual about this."

"Sweetheart, there is nothing casual about my feelings. I promise you that. Casual is a one-night stand. Casual is sex on a first date. Casual is falling into bed with someone you know perfectly well you'll never marry. This is not casual. Okay?"

She sighed. "I know," she said in a low voice, barely above a whisper. "Maybe that's the worst of it."

At the next traffic light, he turned to her, his expression grave. "Liz, do you want to change your mind about tonight? If you do, I'll understand. I want you very badly, but I can wait until you're ready."

The offer hung in the air between them. Liz seriously considered taking him up on it, then realized that not only would it be cowardly, it also was not what she wanted at all, not deep inside where emotions formed.

"I don't want to wait," she said, then added with a kind of quiet desperation, "I just want to be there."

"Me, too, sweetheart. Me, too."

The urgency and longing in Todd's voice got to her. As suddenly as they'd attacked, the butterflies vanished. She was as sure of her feelings for Todd, as sure of what she wanted as she'd ever been of anything in her life. He was a man of warmth and humor and sensitivity. When he cared, he cared with a blind and deep passion. He would always cherish those he held dear, scaling mountains, slaying dragons, if that's what was called for. A growing part of her was ready to relinquish at least some of her independence in order to bask in that loving protectiveness. He was right. There was nothing casual about the feelings between them.

Even with that reassurance, at her front door she fumbled through her purse for the key until Todd finally took over the search. He unerringly found the keys and had them inside the house in less than ten seconds.

It seemed like a lifetime.

Despite the resolution she'd come to in the car, Liz found herself at a loss again the minute they crossed the threshold.

"I think we could both use a glass of wine," Todd said.

Liz nodded. Then her heart sank. "Oh, dear, I don't think I have any."

"No problem," he said, holding up a bottle she hadn't even noticed. "An old Boy Scout is never unprepared."

"I didn't know Boy Scouts drank wine," she said, her sense of humor making a tentative comeback.

"They don't, but that motto stays with them for life. Sit down and I'll get the wine ready."

Liz didn't want to sit down. She didn't want to let Todd out of her sight. If she were alone too long, she had a feeling all her insecurities would come spinning back and take control again. When she was close to him, all she could think about was getting closer. His heat drew her like a fire on a chilly night. His scent was every bit as alluring as the tang of salt on an ocean breeze. His touch . . . ah, yes, his touch had the power to send her senses on a path every bit as thrilling as that of a star hurtling through a midnight sky.

Apparently unaware that she'd followed him, he turned quickly away from the kitchen counter and found her less than an arm's length away. His eyes widened, then sparked with golden fire.

"I didn't want to wait alone," she explained as he put the glasses and wine back on the counter and reached for her.

"You're not alone, sweetheart. Not anymore."

Blunt but gentle fingers tangled in her upswept hair and sent it tumbling down her back. Warm, wine-scented breath whispered a caress along her neck and turned her blood to flame that fired her body from the inside out. Held tight against his body, hip intimately fit to hip, thigh caressing thigh, she trembled and nearly wept with the joy of the sensation. By the time his lips claimed hers, her body had already surrendered, accepting finally that fate had made her his.

"Liz, should we talk?" he said, his breathing ragged, his voice hoarse.

"No more. Not now. I want to feel. I want you to love me, Todd. We've waited so long. Just love me." The last was part demand, part plea. The urgency conveyed itself to him, because he swept her into his arms and carried her through the house, guided by her murmured directions, spurred on by her unrestrained kisses.

At the sight of her brass bed, Todd's eyes smoldered. "Somehow I've always known," he said. "When I've imagined you waiting for me, it's always been in a bed like this."

"I haven't always had this bed," she said, wanting him to know he would be the first to share it. There were no ghosts here. "I bought it after..."

"Ssh. No talk of the past tonight. We're living in the present. There's just you and me and the way we feel when we're together."

With great care and evident fascination he began to remove her clothes. His hands were adept at the task, but it was the expression in his eyes that set off fireworks. There was so much adoration there, so much tenderness. Liz had never felt as beautiful. He took away her shyness and gave her back love.

He took far less care with his own undressing. She wanted to savor the slow revelations as he had with her, but it was as if he'd already expended the last of his self-control. He was bare to the waist in what seemed no more than a single urgent tug of his shirt. Belt and pants followed before she could even begin to delight in the broad expanse of his chest. Dressed only in navy briefs, he pulled her back into his arms. She felt as if she'd come home, after a long, lonely journey. She felt as if heaven might be no more than a kiss away.

The slow, sweet caresses gave way to more demanding touches. With unerring accuracy Todd discovered the secrets to her body. He teased boldly. He stroked with maddening tenderness. And when, at last, he claimed her, it was with a promise on his lips and in his touch. With passion exploding in a burst of rainbow colors, the promise was kept.

Again and again through the timeless night, they found new ways to communicate without words. Todd sighed in contentment as Liz lay curled against his side, her head resting on his shoulder, her hair streaming across his chest. He had known she would be like this. He had known that her sensuality would match his, that she would arouse him beyond his wildest dreams.

Time and again, he had watched her amber eyes darken with passion, lit by an internal flame. With breath held, he had watched her lazy, catlike stretches. Then, unable to resist the tempting curves, he had stroked her until her skin glowed and her body turned demanding. Sheathed in silken heat, he had found release. He had discovered commitment.

The only things he didn't find during the hours when they loved and slept and loved again were the words to tell her how he felt. He talked of love but not permanence. He blamed it on Liz's oft-spoken fear of marriage, but he knew it was his own. The commitment might be there in his heart, but the vows terrified him. They were too easily broken, the heart a long time mending.

It was only seven when he slid from the bed and took a shower. When he came back into the bedroom, a towel wrapped around his hips, Liz was awake, her eyes still heavy-lidded with sleep. She looked magnificent and incredibly tempting. Still. Always.

"You're up early," she observed.

He heard the regret in her voice and grinned. "Believe me, I'd rather be back in that bed with you, but we need to get back to my place."

"Hank's there."

"True, but Sarah's coming back."

"Yes, of course. I'd forgotten." Her voice went flat and the fire in her eyes dimmed.

Todd went to sit on the edge of the bed. He braced his hands on either side of her and leaned down to press a kiss to lips still swollen and sensual from a night of passionate lovemaking. "What's wrong?"

"Who said anything's wrong?"

"Is it Sarah? You're not jealous of her, are you? There's no reason to be. She may be back in my life, but she is still very much the past, romantically speaking. You're my present, my future."

Her arms crept around his neck at that. Her kiss was a little desperate, demanding, hungry, even after so many others. "Make love to me, Todd. Again. I need you so."

His body responded at once to her urging. His head resisted. "We really need . . ."

Her lips were on his shoulders, his chest. Her hands provoked and teased until his protests died. He came alive to her touch, his arousal more urgent than even the first, his need as sharp and demanding as hers. She pulled him to her, crying out her need, seeking something more, luring him beyond past heights until tension shattered into a thousand bits of pleasure that shimmered forever before finally dimming into exhausted contentment.

"I don't think I'll ever move again," he said, sprawled on his back, Liz's leg draped across his.

"It's okay with me. I could stay this way forever."

"Probably not forever," he said practically.

"I suppose sooner or later we'd want food," she conceded.

"Maybe a little wine."

"A swim would be refreshing."

"Maybe a video, an old Katharine Hepburn-Spencer Tracy film."

She lifted herself to one elbow and grinned at him. "I've always said the excitement doesn't last. It's not even twenty-four hours and you want to rent a movie."

"I was thinking long-range. At the moment, I'd settle for one last kiss and breakfast."

"I can manage both of those."

"From you I'll take the kiss. I think we ought to get Hank and Kevin for breakfast. We'll even get Sarah and go someplace with an outdoor terrace and champagne and strawberries."

"Okay," she said agreeably, but her voice went flat on him again.

She was quiet during the breakfast they all shared at an oceanside restaurant on Key Biscayne. Though her smile was warm and intimate whenever he managed to catch her eye, she evaded most of his attempts to draw her into the conversation.

Kevin was slowly beginning to respond to Sarah, reluctantly agreeing to go for a walk along the beach with her. Todd hadn't thought it possible, but Liz went even quieter after that. Fortunately Hank kept up a nonstop conversation on business and the attributes of the various bikini-clad tourists wandering past. Both of them watched Liz uneasily, but neither of them seemed able to reach her. Not even Hank's intentionally blatant, chauvinistic remarks could goad her into a reaction stronger than a mild frown.

To Todd's dismay, the minute they got back to his place she said she had to leave.

"I have a lot of papers to grade and lesson plans to complete," she insisted over his protests.

Troubled but unable to do anything except accept her excuses, Todd said, "I'll call you later."

"Whatever," she said, slipping into her car before he could even kiss her goodbye. He felt his stomach tie into knots as he watched her drive away.

"Hey, buddy, what was that all about?" Hank asked, waiting for him as he walked slowly back toward the house.

"I wish to hell I knew."

"Last night—?"

"Is none of your business," he snapped, heading for the terrace.

Hank followed silently. When they'd been seated for a few minutes, he said, "I'm not trying to pry, you know."

Todd felt like a louse. "Oh, hell, I know you're not. Nothing happened last night that should have sent her scurrying out of here this morning. Quite the contrary, I thought we were well on our way to a new understanding."

"It may be my fault," Sarah offered, coming to join them on the terrace.

Todd shook his head. "I asked her about that. She knows it's over between the two of us. I don't think she's jealous."

"Maybe not of you and me, but what about my relationship with Kevin? From what you've told me she's taken a special interest in him from the beginning. After losing her own child, maybe she's afraid of losing Kevin, too."

Todd groaned as the obviousness of the explanation struck him. "That has to be it. Why the hell didn't I see it?"

"Could be because you thought of yourself as the only important factor in the equation," Sarah chided. "Liz may be looking at the whole package."

"I'd better go talk to her."

Sarah shook her head. "Talking won't convince her, Todd. You're going to have to show her that she's still the most important person in your life and in Kevin's. Actions speak louder than words. It'll be easier when I'm gone."

Todd regarded Sarah with new respect. "You've changed."

She gave him a wry smile. "I told you I'd grown up. About time, don't you think?"

"Better late than never," he said, then stood up. "I think I'll go call Liz. She should be home by now."

He heard Hank's ribald comment as he went into the kitchen. Sarah chuckled. Then he heard Kevin calling out to the two of them to watch him dive into the pool. His world was nearly perfect.

Then he heard Liz's voice, his heart filled to over-flowing and he knew the meaning of true contentment.

Chapter Thirteen

As if he'd guessed the cause of her uneasiness, Todd set out to court Liz over the next few weeks. She recognized all the signs of a man intent on wooing a woman. She found flowers—tiny, delicate orchids, no less—on her desk at school, delivered mysteriously, no doubt by Kevin. Todd took her to romantic dinners in quiet, out-of-the-way restaurants. He took her on moonlit walks on the beach. And he made sure that Kevin was included in many of their outings. The lure of family was once again ensnaring her.

As the Christmas holidays neared, they went shopping together. Using Kevin as the excuse, they spent hours in toy stores, arguing over practicality and educational value versus sheer enjoyment. Todd insisted on a train. Liz picked out a talking computer that helped with spelling and reading. Todd chose a collection of battery-powered toy cars. Liz found videotapes of classic books, then added picture-filled editions of the books, as well. In the end it was clear that Kevin's growing pile of presents was probably as much for them as it was for him.

Two weeks before Christmas Kevin begged to get a tree.

"It's still early," Todd protested. "All the needles will fall off."

"The same tree will still be sitting on the lot a week from now," Liz countered, taking Kevin's side. "By then the needles will be in even worse shape from all that exposure to the sun."

"Tell the truth," Todd retorted with an indulgent smile. "You can't wait, either. I've seen the way your eyes light up at the mall displays. The next thing I know you're going to want to sit on Santa's knee."

She grinned back at him. "An intriguing notion. Think he'd bring me what I want?"

"Perhaps you ought to whisper it in my ear first."

"Hey, you guys, are we gonna get a tree or not?" Kevin inquired testily.

"We'll get the tree," Todd said, casting a look of regret at Liz.

It took hours. They finally found what they wanted at the fourth Christmas tree lot they went to.

"Hey, Dad, I think this is it," Kevin shouted as Liz and Todd examined a small, perfectly formed Scotch pine on the other side of the lot.

"Let's take a look at what he found."

"But this one's just fine," Todd protested.

"Come on, Scrooge."

When they rounded the corner of the last row, they found Kevin standing, hands on hips, staring up in awe at a storybook tree at least ten feet tall and so big around only the largest room would accommodate it. Liz's eyes widened.

"It's beautiful," she breathed softly.

"It's too big. We'd have to move half the furniture."

"Oh, Dad, please. I'll help with the furniture."

"We don't have nearly enough decorations."

"I'll buy some new ones," Liz offered.

Todd thew up his hands in surrender. He turned to the salesman. "I guess we'll take it."

"And the little one," Liz said.

Todd looked bewildered. "The little one? Why two?"

"For my house."

"But you're hardly ever there."

"It would seem too dreary without one."

"I'll go get it," Todd said.

They stopped off at Liz's house and decorated her tree in less than an hour. The efficient, emotionless process reminded her of all the Christmases when Ed had left the decorating to her and barely showed up long enough to exchange presents on Christmas morning. As much as she'd always loved the holidays, Ed had turned them into an ordeal to be gotten through stoically. Laura had been barely old enough to understand what was happening until that last

Christmas. Liz treasured her memories of that day. Her family had come from Indiana, their last visit before the accident and before their own deaths a year later. Even Ed had been more jovial than usual, as they all shared in Laura's wide-eyed amazement.

This year held all the promise of matching that last year with her family. Excitement already teased at her senses as it had when she'd been growing up in Indiana. There was no wintry bite in the air, no pond frozen over for ice-skating, and they hadn't gone traipsing into the countryside to find the tree, but the spirit was there just the same.

On the way to Todd's they stopped to pick up extra strands of lights, colored balls and boxes of icicles for his tree. They turned the night into an impromptu tree-decorating party. Hank came with his latest date. Kevin invited a friend. Liz fixed a huge pot of shrimp gumbo. And carols played on the stereo throughout the evening as they fought over the proper placement of the colored lights, then on the best technique for adding icicles.

When everyone else had left and Kevin had gone to bed, she and Todd sat on the sofa and stared at the blinking lights. 'Silent Night' played softly in the background.

"It's beautiful. If you squint your eyes, all the lights sort of blend together. It's like a kaleidoscope or maybe an impressionist painting," she said, curled contentedly into Todd's arms. When he didn't respond, she poked him gently with her elbow. "Hey, you, don't you think it's beautiful?"

"I don't know," he murmured, running his finger along the back of her neck. "I can't take my eyes off of you."

"Oh, Todd."

Her life, she decided, was just about perfect.

On Friday of the week before Christmas Liz was at the stove, Kevin at the kitchen table doing homework, when Todd came in through the garage. The mall had opened the week before with fireworks displays and sales to tempt even the most jaded shopper. He was simply finishing up the last minute work as the stores settled in. Already, a new project was underway. It would get into full swing the week after New Year's. Hank had already left town for the holidays to visit friends in Maine. Since it was unseasonably hot still in Miami, he had promised to bring back snow for Kevin. Liz knew that Todd had bought tickets for all three of them to go visit the snow instead. The trip was yet another surprise for Kevin. She worried that Kevin was likely to become spoiled, especially with Sarah now doing her best to win him over, but it was not something she felt comfortable discussing with Todd. The status of their relationship was still too uncertain, too impermanent.

"A man could get used to this," Todd said, dropping a kiss on her forehead as he reached into the refrigerator for a beer. He popped the top, took a sip, then lifted the lid of the pot on the stove. "Smells wonderful. What is it?"

"Seafood chowder."

"Any lobster?" he inquired, winking at her.

"Have you checked the price of lobster lately?"

"Oh, is that why you left it out?"

Liz laughed at his determined reminder of the night they'd set the lobsters free in the Keys. "Don't press your luck with me, Mr. Lewis. You'll be eating hot dogs all alone on the patio."

"There's a front moving through. It's cold on the patio."

"Exactly," she said, smacking his hand as it dipped into the salad bowl for another cherry tomato.

"Hey, Dad," Kevin interrupted. "Can you help me with this?"

"What is it?"

"It's a math assignment. You're great at math."

As Todd went to look over Kevin's shoulder, Liz felt a familiar warmth stealing through her. This was what she'd expected to have with Ed, the camaraderie, the laughter, the caring. The last few weeks had been just about perfect, the best she'd ever had. It was all getting to be far too comfortable. How much longer would Todd allow this casual situation to last? How much longer before he began pressing for something more permanent? She loved him. She'd long since admitted that, but every time she thought of marriage, she bumped straight into all of her old insecurities. He seemed to have his share of doubts, as well.

As she watched, Todd straightened, a shuttered expression on his face. "You'll get more out of it, if you try to do it yourself," he said, his tone curt.

"But, Dad," Kevin protested, as Todd threw his empty beer can into the trash can and walked through the door.

"Try, Kevin. If you still can't get it, maybe Liz will help you when she has a minute. I'm going to take a shower before dinner."

"Todd, there's time," she began, but he was already gone. She stared after him, wondering what on earth had gotten into him. He usually didn't press Kevin like that, when he knew how easily the child gave up in the face of school work that seemed beyond him. "Sweetheart, I'll help in a minute. Just let me stir the chowder."

Kevin slammed his book on the floor. "I'm going swimming."

"Kevin!"

Liz stared around the suddenly deserted kitchen. So much for a cozy evening at home.

Dinner was a tense affair. Todd looked guilty. Kevin sulked. And she foolishly tried to keep a conversation going despite it. She might as well have been talking to herself. After about twenty minutes of this strained atmosphere, Kevin asked to be excused.

"Go," Todd said tightly.

"What has gotten into you?" Liz snapped. "When you came in tonight, you were in a perfectly good mood. Now you're growling around like a bear with a thorn stuck in its paw. All Kevin did was ask for a little help with his homework. You didn't have to make a federal case out of it. You know he still has difficulty with math when it involves word problems."

He glared at her and said nothing. She scowled right back. "Don't try intimidating me, Todd Lewis. I can always leave," she said, proving the point by getting to her feet.

"That's why you like it this way, isn't it? When things get tough, you can still walk out."

Stunned by the harsh accusation, she ripped off the apron she was wearing and grabbed her purse. As she passed his chair, he caught her wrist.

"Don't go."

"Let go of me," she bit out, her teeth clenched.

"Liz, please."

She sighed. "Can you give me one single reason I should stay?"

"I want you here. I'm sorry for what I said and I'm sorry for spoiling the evening."

"I'm less concerned about having the evening spoiled than I am about what's wrong with you."

"I can't explain. It's just that sometimes my temper gets the better of me. It's as if our whole relationship is all tied up with helping Kevin. Sometimes I wonder what will happen when the school year ends and he's no longer your project."

"My project? Is that what you think this is all about?"

"Isn't it the truth? Haven't you set your life up so that it works in neat little nine-month cycles? No one kid gets too close for too long. June rolls around and there's a natural break, no messy emotional loose ends. This year it was Kevin. Sometimes I wonder if you'd put up with me at all, if you weren't so worried about him."

Liz was flabbergasted. "Todd, how can you even think that? How can you resent the fact that I care about Kevin? He's your son. He's not your competitor. I have enough love to go around."

"I know that," he said defensively. "And it's not that I resent Kevin. Hell, I don't know what it is. It was a long day."

"No longer than most and you were in a great mood when you came through the door. Please, tell me what's really wrong."

Todd's chair scraped the tiles as he shoved it back angrily. He threw his napkin on the table. "Just forget it. I'm going out for awhile."

"Leaving me here with Kevin? I don't think so. I'm not your hired babysitter, Todd." Once again she grabbed her purse off the kitchen counter and stalked through the house and out the front door, setting off the burglar alarm in the process. She heard the damn thing ringing until she turned off the street.

The next morning Liz set out at dawn to drive to the Keys. Suddenly she needed desperately to see Ann. She needed her friend's advice and warmth and the crazy exuberance of her household. She arrived while the kitchen seemed to be under siege. No one heard her knock, so she finally just walked in.

"Hi, Liz," Tracy greeted her without the slightest evidence of surprise. Tracy was the oldest of the current brood, a sixteen-year-old who'd been a victim of abuse. Ann had taken her in when she was thirteen, skinny and terrified. She had blossomed into a lovely young woman.

"Want some cereal? Juice?" she asked.

"Just coffee, if there's any made."

"Sure thing. Have a seat if you can find one. Josh, you're through. Move it and give Liz your chair."

"That's okay. I can stand for awhile. It's a long drive."

Josh grinned at her. Dark-haired and dark-eyed, he had been sullen and difficult when he'd arrived, sent to Ann as an alternative to becoming enmeshed in the juvenile justice system. It had taken the better part of a year for Ann to penetrate his brooding moods and show him that there were more positive ways of getting attention than breaking the law.

"You'd better sit," he advised. "Tracy's decided she's boss for the day. She gets nasty if we don't follow her orders."

Liz found herself grinning, despite the weight that seemed to have lodged in her chest the night before. "Then by all means, I'll sit. Is Ann around?"

"Last time I saw her she was trying to persuade Melissa to give up her blanket long enough for it to be washed," Josh said as Tracy handed Liz a mug of coffee. "I've got to get out of here to cut the grass before soccer practice. I'll go look for her."

"Thanks, Josh." She pushed cereal bowls and dirty glasses out of the way, so there'd be room for the coffee mug. Once she'd been settled, the other kids still at the table seemed to forget all about her. She sat quietly and let the noisy teasing ebb and flow around her. Even when tempers flared it was all so alive, so filled with energy and joy. It made her own house seem even quieter.

A few minutes later, Ann breezed into the room, dropped a kiss on Liz's forehead and set about hurrying all the children out the door to do their various chores. "Tracy, watch the little ones. Try to see that they don't fall in the ocean and drown."

She fixed herself a cup of tea, then sat down. "So, what brings you to visit so early on Saturday morning?"

"I just felt like a drive."

Ann directed a sharp look at her. "You hate traveling on U.S. 1 almost as much as I hated living in Miami. Try another one on me."

"It's Todd."

"You're in love with him?"

Liz nodded, not at all surprised that Ann had guessed. That's what Liz loved about her. She was smart and intuitive. Also, she wasted no words, just offered a blunt summation that zeroed in on the heart of the problem.

"And that's a problem? Why? It's about time you admitted it. I've known it for weeks now."

"That's because you're an objective observer. I've been fighting it."

"Are you crazy? He's gorgeous, generous, sensitive and he loves you. Or doesn't he?" She shook her head. "I don't know what I'm bothering to ask for. He's just as starry-eyed as you are."

"He says he does."

Ann put her elbows on the table and leaned forward. "Okay, Liz, that's enough double-talk. Sweetheart, I'm a psychologist, not a mind reader. So far, everything you've said adds up to bliss. You don't look blissful."

"I'm miserable. There's something he's not telling me. We had this huge fight last night, because he wouldn't be straight with me. Maybe he's still in love with his ex-wife. Maybe he just can't figure out a way to break it to me."

"Didn't you tell me that you played hostess to her at Thanksgiving? Living with a zillion kids under the age of eighteen, I may not be up on all the current social graces, but I sincerely doubt that Todd would have had the two of you in the same room if he were still hot for his ex."

"I don't think he was . . . then."

"Has anything happened to suggest he's changed his mind. Is he making late-night calls to her? Has he taken off on any unexplained business trips? Found any lipstick on his collar?"

Liz laughed despite her gloomy mood. "When you put it that way, it does seem pretty farfetched. That still doesn't explain this weird mood he's been in. Last night Kevin asked for help with his homework and the next thing I knew Todd had stomped out of the kitchen. Nothing I said or did made any difference. He wouldn't talk about it."

Ann seemed to go perfectly still. "I see."

"Well, dammit, I don't see."

"Did you try to talk to him about it?"

"Yes. He just snapped my head off. He went on some crazy tirade about me making Kevin my project for the year. He thinks I'm already gearing up to get the two of them out of my life."

"Any truth to that?"

"No. It took me a long time to admit I loved him. I sure as hell don't want to walk away from him now."

"Then why aren't you in Miami working this out with him, instead of down here talking to me."

Liz managed a wavering grin. "Because you don't yell at me."

Ann grinned back. "Stick around."

"On second thought, I seem to feel this desperate need to head north."

"Smart decision." She reached over and held Liz's hand. "Talk. Don't attack. Secrets are rarely revealed when everyone's yelling at the top of their lungs."

She turned a penetrating gaze on Ann. A couple of earlier comments suddenly clicked. "Do you know something about this?"

"I didn't say that. I was speaking in generalities."

Liz shook her head slowly. "I don't buy that for a minute. And the only reason I won't press you on it is because I know all the rules about confidentiality."

She waited for some indication that her noble restraint had hit its mark. Ann only repeated, "Talk to him. He'll come around. And no matter what, remember the stakes. Good love is hard to find."

"Maybe I should just hang around here. You're supposed to see him today, aren't you? Doesn't Kevin have an appointment?"

"He did. Todd called a little while before you got here to cancel."

"Oh, hell."

Ann shrugged resignedly. "One missed appointment is not the end of the world. In fact, right now, I'd suggest you leave that subject alone. Stick to what's happening between you and Todd, for once. He may need to know he comes first with you."

Liz thought about Ann's advice all the way home. An hour later she had just gotten out of the tub, when the doorbell rang. She wrapped herself in a terry-cloth robe, wound a towel around her wet hair and peered through the peephole. Todd was standing on the doorstep, his expression subdued.

"Can you give me one good reason to open this door?" she said, though there wasn't much anger behind the taunt.

"I love you."

Her remaining irritation slid away. "Not bad," she said, swinging open the door. "What'll you do for an encore?"

He pulled her into his arms and slanted his mouth across hers. His tongue teased. His rough hands slid inside her robe and caressed her breasts, his thumbs rubbing the nipples until they hardened into sensitive buds. Liz melted. Her knees went limp and she clung to him.

"Don't ever walk out on me again," he pleaded, his voice hoarse and urgent. "Please."

"I'm sorry. It was a cowardly thing to do. I should have stayed so we could talk it out. Can we do it now?"

"Not right now, Liz. I want to take you away. I want to go someplace where it's just the two of us, someplace where we can concentrate on us."

Ann's comments echoed through her mind. "Does this sudden desire to get away have to do with what you said earlier about our needs getting all twisted up with Kevin's?"

"Partly. Mostly, though, there are things I want you to know about me, things I haven't been able to tell you before."

"And we need to go away for you to be able to do that?" she said, puzzled.

Todd's mouth curved into a rueful expression. "Maybe I just want you to be someplace where you can't run away so easily."

"There's nothing you can say that would be so awful that I'd run from you."

"I'd like to believe that, Liz. God knows I need to believe that."

"You can," she said, increasingly concerned by his odd mood. "I love you. I'm scared, especially knowing that there is some secret between us, but that doesn't mean I intend to run from my feelings or from yours."

"Wait before you say that. Wait until you know everything."

"We're all going away next week."

"That's just it, we're all going."

"Don't you think we'll be able to find time alone?"

"I suppose."

"Todd, we'll make the time. That's a promise."

He held her then, the embrace surprisingly desperate. The renewed certainty that there were emotions plaguing Todd that threatened their happiness scared her to death. Suddenly the entire holiday season, which she'd been anticipating with such excitement, seemed threatening. Would they still be together beyond the New Year?

Chapter Fourteen

Liz's growing despair almost ruined the holidays for her. She was terrified to let herself feel too much for fear it was all going to be snatched away from her again. She wrapped presents for Todd and Kevin and went to parties with her coworkers and Todd's friends with a vague but no less disquieting sense that it was all for the last time. Her mood communicated itself to Todd and he grew increasingly quiet.

In the already tense atmosphere, it wasn't surprising that they got into frequent quarrels over inconsequential things. The bickering escalated into a full-scale battle when she asked about inviting his family to spend Christmas Day with them. She knew they lived in Boca Raton, but very little else.

"Wouldn't they like to be here on Christmas morning? They could drive down on Christmas Eve. There's plenty of room for them."

"No."

"Todd, it's Christmas. Families should be together."

"Not mine."

"Tell me why."

"It's none of your damned business why. The point is I don't want them here. Now stop bugging me about it." He stalked out of the house, slamming the door behind him.

Furious and hurt, she turned around to see Kevin standing on the terrace, his whole body shaking. "Is Dad leaving?"

Liz was shocked by the panic in his eyes, the absolute terror that radiated from him. "You mean for good?"

He nodded, still trembling. She knelt down and gathered him close. "Oh, sweetheart, of course not. I just upset him. That's all. He'll be back."

"When he and Mom fought, she didn't come back."

"This is very different."

"You asked him about my grandparents, didn't you?" he said.

"Yes." She wondered at his oddly accusing tone.

"You shouldn't have done that. He doesn't like them. They came here once and he yelled at them. They didn't ever come back."

Liz sighed. Another secret. Would they never end? Could they survive them?

Despite her doubts and fears, on Christmas Eve she gave herself a stern lecture on wasting the moment. She determinedly allowed herself to indulge in the luxury of being part of a family again. She set out to make the night special. If it was going to end, it would be with only the best of memories.

After a dinner in a favorite neighborhood restaurant, they drove north to see the gigantic Christmas tree in Lantana. Kevin could hardly contain himself. He'd been convinced that no tree could possibly be bigger than theirs. They followed that with a visit to a house near Todd's that put on an annual display of holiday scenes complete with animated figures and enough lights to dazzle children of all ages. Kevin was enchanted. Liz felt her own spirits rise.

The transformation was almost complete by the time they went to a midnight service. Stars glittered brightly. The air, though hardly wintry, had turned brisk enough for sweaters and jackets. At the church they were surrounded by people she had come to know or at least recognize over the past few months of being at Todd's. With the Nativity acted out in front of the candlelit altar, she found herself slowly responding to the carols and the joyous atmosphere. She left the service with a renewed sense of hope.

Getting Kevin to bed was the toughest task of the night. He no longer believed in Santa Claus, but that didn't prevent him from wanting to lurk about in the living room just in case the old guy showed up. When he'd finally been convinced that leaving cookies and milk on the coffee table would be incentive enough for Santa or whatever elves were delivering the presents, he went to bed. Todd and Liz spent the next two hours assembling the train set under the tree.

Drinking eggnog and arguing over the arrangement of the village prolonged the process.

"I'm the developer. I know all about land use," Todd grumbled.

"I want the church next to the train station," Liz insisted.

"Have you ever been to a train station? They're always in the worst part of town."

"All the more reason ours should have something beautiful nearby." She grinned. "Besides, they both need an electrical connection and we only have one."

Todd groaned. "So much for urban planning."

On Christmas morning Kevin was up by five-thirty. Todd sent him straight back to bed again, but by six, he'd given up. Half asleep, he and Liz sat on the sofa and watched as Kevin's excitement mounted with each present. Hugs were doled out with enthusiastic frequency. Squeals of delight mingled with the sound of the train whistle and cars racing across the tile floor. It had been years since Liz had heard so much noise at that hour of the morning. The nostalgia choked her. The reality made her feel complete.

Kevin had done his own Christmas shopping. He had found lace-edged handkerchiefs embroidered with her monogram. He was practically bouncing up and down on the sofa, as she opened them. "See," he enthused, "they're just like the ones you always have in school."

"They're lovely. The perfect present."

"Now mine," Todd said, handing her a large box.

When she ripped away the paper, she saw the name of an exclusive boutique in Mayfair, an elegant collection of shops in the heart of Coconut Grove.

"Todd," she protested, her fingers caressing the embossed gold foil label. Even the label was probably fourteen-karat gold, she thought nervously.

"Don't say a word until you've opened it. It's something I wanted you to have and I won't take no for an answer."

Inside, amidst layers of tissue paper, she found the most beautiful dress she'd ever seen. Ankle-length green satin, it was draped to leave one shoulder bare. The single strap was held together with a rhinestone clasp. At least she hoped those were only rhinestones glittering up at her. It was elegant, sexy and totally impractical for a schoolteacher.

"Wow!" Kevin said.

"You said it," she said in an awed whisper.

"Put it on," Kevin said. "I want to see."

She shook her head. "I can't. Todd, it's lovely, but I'll never..."

"You will," he said adamantly. "Remember we have a date in Maine for New Year's Eve and that's the dress I want you to wear."

* * *

Although Liz had worried about the extravagance, the trip to Maine was exactly the vacation they all needed. With snow on the ground, a huge fireplace in the lodge and nothing to do all day but enjoy the spectacular scenery, ski a little or simply sit back and read all the books she'd put aside during the fall school term, Liz was in heaven.

On New Year's Eve afternoon she was almost finished with a Pulitzer Prize-winning biography, when Todd came back from taking Kevin to town for a new pair of ski boots to replace the ones he'd outgrown. He leaned down to kiss her.

"Umm, nice," she observed, "but your nose is cold."

"So's the rest of me. Care to warm me up?"

"It's the middle of the afternoon and your son is in the next room."

"No, he's not. Hank and his date took him for the rest of the day."

"What a wonderful friend," she noted.

"I thought you'd think so."

"Sometimes I wonder if we'd ever have a moment alone, if it weren't for Hank."

"I think we owe it to him to make his sacrifice worthwhile," he said, pulling her into his arms. His hands were already sliding under her ski sweater to caress and tease.

"Absolutely," she concurred, fumbling with the zipper on his jacket.

It took far more time to disrobe in the icy climate, but the loss of time was more than compensated for with the heightened sense of anticipation. As layers were peeled away and kisses stolen, the sweet tension mounted in Liz. Even before Todd had her clothes off and cast aside, he had teased her to a shattering climax.

"Not fair," she murmured, clinging to him and seeking the masculine nipples that were buried in swirls of dark blond hair that matted his chest.

"You didn't enjoy that?" he said, groaning himself as her tongue teased the hard little bud.

"I wanted you with me, inside me."

"It doesn't always have to be that way. Sometimes I just want to give you pleasure. I want you to take everything I can offer you and let me watch as you reach the crest."

"Then let me do the same," she said, drawing him down in front of the fire, her hands already at work, stroking the supple muscles that spanned his chest, the flat plane of his belly with its tiny, sensitive indentation. Her tongue flicked in and out in a sensual rhythm that had Todd already breathing hard by the time she reached lower. At her sure, insistent touch, he moaned with pleasure.

"I see what you mean," he said on a ragged sigh. "I want you with me."

A slow smile spread across her face. "I'm right here," she said and settled on him, riding him with wild abandon until they both reached a destination far beyond their dreams.

They were lying together on the rug in front of the fire, still bathed in the afterglow of lovemaking that grew more satisfying each time they were in each other's arms, when Todd murmured, "What did you do today?"

"You mean before this?"

"Umm."

"It wasn't nearly as interesting."

"Tell me anyway."

"I was reading." She described the biography. "The writer is excellent and the man it's about is someone I think you'd really admire. You ought to read it, when I'm finished. It's fascinating."

She felt Todd's arms stiffen at once. Twisting, she scanned his face. "What's wrong?"

He sighed heavily and released her. "I suppose now is as good a time as any to tell you."

Cold without his arms around her, she reached for a blanket. Her heart thudded ominously. "Tell me what?"

"I can't read the book, Liz," he said bluntly. "I can't read any book. At least not easily. I'm dyslexic. Ann's done a little work with me over the last couple of months and coupled with what I've managed to do myself, I'm a little better, but it will always be a struggle."

She saw the uncertainty written all over his face, the fear that his announcement was going to change something between them. That vulnerability broke her heart. At the same time, she felt betrayed. He'd kept something so basic about himself from her, something that would have told her so much about him and about his protectiveness of Kevin. The fact that he hadn't trusted her with his secret hurt. Worse, she realized now that Ann had known. That only compounded her feeling that for all the love he'd professed, Todd hadn't loved her enough.

"Why didn't you feel you could tell me?" she asked, her heart aching.

"I was afraid it would change things. When you and I met, I was still in a lot of pain over Sarah's rejection. I was convinced that she'd turned away from Kevin and from me because we were less than perfect. I know it sounds crazy, especially after the way she's been acting lately, but that's the way I felt at the time. I couldn't bear the thought of losing you the same way."

"But you told Ann."

"I didn't tell her, at least not willingly. She guessed that very first day we went down there."

That didn't make her feel any better. "My God, I must have been blind," she said pulling away and going to get a robe. When she was covered, she sat huddled in a chair and went over all the signs she'd missed before.

"That's why you never helped Kevin with his homework," she said. "Why you got so angry that night he asked you to look at his math. Those were word problems."

He nodded.

"And that's why you never looked at your mail when I was around. That's why Hank was usually the one who went over the terms of your contracts, rather than the other way around. It never made sense before that you were in charge, that you made the business decisions, but he worked on the contracts. He knows, too."

"Don't say it like he's part of some conspiracy. We grew up together. He's always known. I'm not sure I'd have gotten through high school without Hank. In his way, he coached me through it as best he could."

Liz felt numb. "I want to go home," she said. "I have a lot of thinking to do."

Todd's expression hardened. "I knew this would happen. It's the reason I didn't tell you sooner. I knew you'd walk away from me."

She shook her head. "I'm not walking away because you're dyslexic, Todd. That's something you couldn't help. I admire the way you've overcome it, the way you've gone on to make a success of yourself despite the difficulties. I'm leaving because I can't stay in a relationship without trust. It just won't work. I'm going home."

With the same stoic expression she'd seen all too often on Kevin's face, Todd nodded and left her alone to pack. No protests. No pleas. Just calm acceptance, as if he'd known all along what her decision would be.

In a daze, she called the airlines, made a reservation for the next flight back to Miami and packed her bags. She was getting ready to call for a bellboy, when there was a knock on the door.

"Liz, it's Hank. Can we talk?"

Reluctantly, she opened the door. "I'm running late. I have a cab waiting."

"If you're determined to go, I'll drive you. We can talk on the way."

"I don't think so. I'm not sure I can bear to listen to a lengthy defense of what Todd has done. Whatever you want to say, say it here."

"Dammit, what exactly has he done? He hasn't lied or cheated or betrayed you. Not really. He's acted human. He held back a part of himself that was less than perfect because he was afraid it would change the way you felt about him. Now you're proving him right. You're leaving. I thought you were different. We both did."

"Dammit, I told him I'm not going because he has difficulty reading. I'm going because he didn't trust me enough to tell me."

"If every person you'd ever really loved had abandoned you and you were convinced that they'd all done it because you couldn't live up to their expectations, would you openly admit it to the next person who came along? Especially when you could manage to cover up the flaw? Is what Todd did any different from a woman who wears makeup to disguise a birthmark for fear that it will scare off a potential suitor? Is that a lie? Or what about the woman who wears a certain style of clothes not because they're stylish but because they hide a flaw in her figure. Sure, sooner or later the truth comes out. If the relationship grows the man sees the birthmark or the heavy thighs or the small bust, but by then he's also gotten to know the person inside that flawed body.''

''But if the man was so superficial that the birthmark or thighs or the size of the bustline would have scared him away, is that the sort of man she should want?''

''Liz, in the beginning most relationship are superficial. They're based on all sorts of preconceived notions of what we expect true beauty or intelligence or sensitivity to be. There are very few of us who don't try to minimize our flaws and emphasize our good qualities, when we meet people for the first time. Hell, when you go on a job interview, your resumé covers all the successes. You don't spend a hell of a lot of time discussing the classes you almost failed or the fact that four days out of five you couldn't afford to dress in the suit you chose for the interview.''

''Then you think that what Todd did was okay?''

''I think it was human. Has he ever told you the way his parents treated him? Did he ever explain how his brilliant father, a man at the top of the legal profession, turned his back on him once he'd decided Todd would never be able to get through law school?''

''That's why he doesn't see his parents?'' she said in a shaky voice.

''Yes. They gave up on him, too. Imagine what that does to a kid in his teens when he's already struggling with just growing up. Then his wife walks out, too. Probably not for the same reason, but it's another rejection just the same. Is it any wonder he's cautious with the truth? Just promise me you'll try to see it from his point of view. The man's nuts about you.''

"You're a good friend, Hank. I'm glad he's always had you to make up for the losses, to stand by him. He told me what you did for him in school.''

Hank feigned shock, allowing a tiny flicker of amusement to spark in his eyes. "He didn't. He promised he would never tell about that date I arranged for him.''

Liz laughed. "Still can't admit it, can you?''

"Admit what?''

"That you're a terrific guy.''

"I know *that*. I thought you wanted me to tell you what happened on the date.''

"Get out of here, Hank.''

"On my way.''

At the door he stopped and looked back. "You'll never find a finer man, Liz. And I doubt if there will ever be one who'll love you more.''

She sighed. "I know that. I'm just not sure it's enough.''

All the way to the airport, she thought about what Hank had said. She recalled the look in Todd's eyes when he'd told her the truth, that mixture of hope and anxiety. And then she remembered the despair when she'd done exactly as he'd anticipated and turned away from him. The horrible lump in her throat seemed to grow larger with each mile she put between her and Todd.

"Turn the cab around," she finally told the driver.

"You forget something? You'll never make your flight, if we go back."

"I almost forgot the most important thing of all," she said. "And if I don't go back, I may lose it forever."

He shrugged, obviously used to impulsive, scatterbrained tourists. "It's your nickel on the meter, lady."

When she got back to the hotel, she made sure that Todd was out of the room before going back. Once inside, she showered and changed into the green gown he'd given her for Christmas. She was just putting the finishing touches on her hair when she heard the door to the room open.

Todd came in and sank down into the chair in front of the fireplace. She'd never seen him look quite so sad, so utterly defeated. Knowing that she was responsible made her heart ache.

Taking a deep breath, she put a smile on her face and stepped into the room. When Todd looked up and saw her, his shock registered in his eyes.

"I thought you'd left," he said cautiously.

"I had. I came back."

"Why?"

"It's New Year's Eve and I had this date I didn't want to miss."

"Anyone I know?"

"I'm not sure. He's tall, handsome, incredibly sexy and quite possibly the nicest man I've ever known."

"Sounds like a helluva guy. What happens after to-night? Do you have any plans?"

"That's up to my date."

Todd didn't even attempt to hide the anguish she'd put him through. Not even the teasing lightened his mood. "Liz, I can't take you walking out on me again. If you don't plan to stay, go now."

"Like I said, what happens next is up to you."

She saw the heat flare in his eyes, the first hint of hope. "You could start by taking off the dress," he suggested.

She allowed herself a slight chuckle. "Oh, no, you don't. I just put it on."

He stood up and came closer. He ran one finger along the low-cut neckline, leaving a trail of fire across her skin. "There's not much to it," he observed. "How much trouble could it be to take it off, then put it back on again? I'll even help."

"What a guy!"

He reached around her and worked the zipper down. The slow rasp sent shivers along the curve of her spine. "I love you," he whispered, kissing the hollow at the base of her neck. " I missed you."

"I was only gone for an hour or so."

"But it could have been a lifetime."

"I'd have come to my senses sooner or later."

"What made you change your mind?"

"Something Hank said."

"Hank came to talk to you about me? What did he say?"

"He said I'd never meet a finer man."

"Probably true," he teased immodestly.

"He said no one would ever love me more."

"Definitely true."

"He also mentioned something about a date he arranged for you."

"He what?"

"That, of course, was the clincher. Hank Riley is not going to direct your social life."

"Does that mean you're going to take me out of circulation?"

"I suppose I'll have to."

"Quite a sacrifice you're willing to make."

"Keep it in mind, when you're taking out the trash. That should even things up rather nicely."

He sighed. "I can't believe New Year's Eve is actually working out the way I'd planned. You're here. You're wearing the dress I'd imagined you in." He glanced down at the pool of green satin at her feet. "Well, almost wearing it, anyway. It seems like there was something else."

"Something else?"

"The ring. There's supposed to be a ring."

"An engagement ring? You actually have an engagement ring?"

"I have a wedding ring, too, but Hank's holding on to that. I didn't want to lose it before the wedding. Thank goodness he didn't mention that while he was trying to be persuasive."

"My head seems to be spinning here. What exactly did you have in mind for tonight?"

"Just the proposal. I figured we'd have to wait for the wedding."

"I'm glad you realized that. It takes time to plan a wedding."

"Oh, it's all planned. I just couldn't figure out how to get you to take a blood test without telling you what I was up to."

"You were incredibly confident, weren't you?"

"Not for a minute, sweetheart. I've been praying since the day we met."

Epilogue

The late afternoon sunlight streaming in the nursery window cast a golden shadow over the room he and Hank had added to the house barely in the nick of time. Fascinated, Todd stood in the doorway feeling his chest constrict in awe at the sight of Liz seated in the old-fashioned rocker, breast bared as their baby suckled, one tiny hand resting on the creamy mound.

"How are my two girls today?" he asked softly, not wanting to disturb the age-old serenity of the intimate moment between mother and child, but needing to feel a part of it.

Liz lifted her head and smiled. The radiance of that smile lit the room, welcoming him. "Why not come and see for yourself. Your daughter is a greedy little thing. She must have gotten it from you.''

''I'd trade places with her in a minute,'' he said in a choked voice. His eyes met Liz's and caught the smoldering heat that always set him on fire.

They had been married more than a year now and that sharp pang of desire hadn't diminished. If anything, the intensity of his feelings had grown, almost overwhelming him at times. His life was fuller, richer than he'd ever imagined possible.

As he watched, Liz put the baby over her shoulder, patted her back, then held her up for him to take. Amy smelled of talcum powder and felt a little bit like heaven in his arms. He wondered if he'd ever taken the time to enjoy Kevin as much when he was an infant and Sarah had still been there to care for him. Probably not. It was only after she'd gone that he'd grown truly close to his son.

''Maybe she'll actually nap long enough for me to get a decent dinner on the table,'' Liz said hopefully, fastening her blouse.

''I can think of better ways to spend the time,'' he said, holding the baby in the crook of his arm and grinning suggestively at his wife.

''Kevin will be home from baseball practice in twenty minutes.''

''Clock-watcher,'' he chided.

''It's a good thing one of us is.''

''There's still time for a shower.''

''Only if you take it alone.''

"Surely there's something we can manage in twenty minutes."

She came to stand beside him as he put the baby into her crib. Her arm looped around his waist and she leaned against him, soft and warm and desirable. "We can stand here and admire our handiwork."

He felt a familiar silly grin of satisfaction slip into place. "We did do a good job, didn't we? Amy is quite possibly the most beautiful baby ever born. She will no doubt grow up to be Miss America." He brushed a light, hopeful kiss across Liz's lips. "Want to see if we can do it again?"

"Oh, beautiful or not, I think one baby in diapers at a time is quite enough, thank you very much. Why don't we go into the kitchen and try to get your mind on other things."

"My mind has rarely been on other things since I met you."

"And here I thought Hank was the one with the overactive libido."

"Speaking of Hank, we had a meeting today. We had to make some decisions about the jobs we have lined up. We decided he'd take the one down in the Keys. He'll be down there for the next few months until the mall is complete."

"Is he going to commute?"

"Not if he can help it. It's pretty far down. He'd even be better off in Key West, if he has to commute from someplace. He's looking for a house or condo to rent for four or five months. Unfortunately, it's the height of the tourist season, so he's not having a lot of luck. Everything's either booked or outrageously expensive."

He caught a sudden gleam of mischief in Liz's eyes. "I recognize that look. What are you thinking?"

"What about Ann's place?"

"What about it?"

"It's only a few miles from the mall. He could stay there. A couple of the kids could double up for a short time."

"Hank hates kids."

Liz grinned. "So he says."

Todd began to understand the perverse scheme that was forming in his wife's devious mind. "Ann's far too independent, far too opinionated," he noted with a glimmer of satisfaction. "She'd drive him crazy. They fought all through the wedding rehearsal."

"Exactly."

"I love it. Think she'll go along with it, though? She called him a chauvinistic jerk at the reception."

"All we have to do is explain how lonely he is, how desperate for a place to stay. Ann has never turned down a stray in her life, especially one in need of reforming."

Todd's laughter boomed through the house. The baby whimpered. He fought to control his delighted reaction to the prospect of Hank Riley and Ann Davies in close proximity.

"I give 'em twenty-four hours."

Liz shook her head solemnly, though her eyes flashed with amusement. "I'm betting on a lifetime."

* * * * *

Watch for Hank and Ann's story in
TEA AND DESTINY, a Silhouette Special
Edition coming this spring!

A compelling novel of deadly revenge and passion
from bestselling international
romance author Penny Jordan

POWER PLAY

Eleven years had passed but the
terror of that night was something
Pepper Minesse would never
forget. Fueled by revenge against
the four men who had brutally
shattered her past, she set in
motion a deadly plan to destroy
their futures.

Available in February!

Penny Jordan

SPP-1A

SILHOUETTE DESIRE™

presents

AUNT EUGENIA'S TREASURES
by CELESTE HAMILTON

Liz, Cassandra and Maggie are the honored recipients of Aunt Eugenia's heirloom jewels…but Eugenia knows the real prizes are the young women themselves. Read about Aunt Eugenia's quest to find them everlasting love. Each book shines on its own, but together, they're priceless!

Available in December:
THE DIAMOND'S SPARKLE (SD #537)

Altruistic Liz Patterson wants nothing to do with Nathan Hollister, but as the fast-lane PR man tells Liz, love is something he's willing to take *very* slowly.

Available in February:
RUBY FIRE (SD #549)

Impulsive Cassandra Martin returns from her travels… ready to rekindle the flame with the man she never forgot, Daniel O'Grady.

Available in April:
THE HIDDEN PEARL (SD #561)

Cautious Maggie O'Grady comes out of her shell…and glows in the precious warmth of love when brazen Jonah Pendleton moves in next door.

Look for these titles wherever Silhouette books are sold, or purchase your copy by sending your name, address and zip or postal code, along with a check or money order for $2.50 for each book ordered, plus 75¢ postage and handling, payable to Silhouette Reader Service to:

In U.S.A.	In Canada
901 Fuhrmann Blvd.	P.O. Box 609
P.O. Box 1396	Fort Erie, Ontario
Buffalo, NY 14269-1396	L2A 5X3

Please specify book title(s) with your order.

SD-AET-1R

You'll flip . . . your pages won't!
Read paperbacks *hands-free* with

Book Mate · I

The perfect "mate" for all your romance paperbacks

Traveling · Vacationing · At Work · In Bed · Studying · Cooking · Eating

Perfect size for all standard paperbacks, this wonderful invention makes reading a pure pleasure! Ingenious design holds paperback books OPEN and FLAT so even wind can't ruffle pages— leaves your hands free to do other things. Reinforced, wipe-clean vinyl-covered holder flexes to let you turn pages without undoing the strap . . . supports paperbacks so well, they have the strength of hardcovers!

Pages turn WITHOUT opening the strap

SEE-THROUGH STRAP

Reinforced back stays flat

Built in bookmark

BOOK MARK

BACK COVER HOLDING STRIP

10 x 7¼ opened.
Snaps closed for easy carrying, too

Available now. Send your name, address, and zip code, along with a check or money order for just $5.95 + .75¢ for postage & handling (for a total of $6.70) payable to Reader Service to:

Reader Service
Bookmate Offer
901 Fuhrmann Blvd.
P.O. Box 1396
Buffalo, N.Y. 14269-1396

Offer not available in Canada
*New York and Iowa residents add appropriate sales tax.

BM-G

At long last, the books you've been waiting for
by one of America's top romance authors!

DIANA PALMER

DUETS

Ten years ago Diana Palmer published her very first
romances. Powerful and dramatic, these gripping tales
of love are everything you have come to expect from
Diana Palmer.

In March, some of these titles will be available again in
DIANA PALMER DUETS—a special three-book collection. Each book will have two wonderful stories plus an
introduction by the author. You won't want to miss them!

Book 1
SWEET ENEMY
LOVE ON TRIAL

Book 2
STORM OVER THE LAKE
TO LOVE AND CHERISH

Book 3
IF WINTER COMES
NOW AND FOREVER

 *Silhouette Books* ®

DP-1

Silhouette Intimate Moments®

Available now...it's time for

TIMES CHANGE
Nora Roberts

Jacob Hornblower is determined to stop his brother, Caleb, from making the mistake of his life—but his timing's off, and he encounters Sunny Stone instead. Their passion is timeless—but will this mismatched couple learn to share their tomorrows?

Don't miss Silhouette Intimate Moments #317

Get your copy now—while there's still time!

If you missed TIME WAS (IM #313) and want to read about Caleb's romantic adventure through time, send your name, address, zip or postal code, along with a check or money order for $2.95, plus 75¢ postage and handling, payable to Silhouette Reader Service to:

In Canada
P.O. Box 609
Fort Erie, Ontario
L2A 5X3

In U.S.A.
901 Fuhrmann Blvd.
P.O. Box 1396
Buffalo, NY 14269-1396

Please specify book title with your order.